"Hello, Trixie."

Tessa slammed on the brakes. Her heart leaped in her chest as she saw the man's face in the mirror. She gripped the steering wheel, scenarios of stalkers and what they did to their victims running through her head.

Then she realized the significance of what the man had said.

Trixie. He'd said *Trixie*. There was only one person in the world who'd ever called her that. It was his pet name for her. Too stunned to speak, she stared into the rearview mirror at Frankie Hamilton. At least, she thought it must be him. He bore little resemblance to the boy she'd known. The mixed-up boy for whom she'd almost thrown away her future.

Dear Reader,

Welcome to my twentieth Harlequin Superromance novel. I hope you enjoy my latest tale, and especially the characters I've created. The idea for this book came to me when I was contemplating the nature of marriage. With divorce rates high, and young people staying single longer, or forever, I wanted to write a story about the enduring nature of marriage, even if the couple runs into problems they think they can't overcome.

A central question in plotting was, when two people love each other deeply and have built a life together, what could pull them apart? To me, most sins are forgivable. In any relationship, people let each other down. They also grow and change from who they were when they took their vows, and this growth doesn't always occur at the same rate for both. Having been married for over three decades—I'll be celebrating the thirty-fifth anniversary with my own personal hero right when this book comes out—I know the ups and downs of relationships. I also know that trusting someone implicitly, even after a difficult time, is a true joy. It's worth working toward.

In *Tell Me No Lies*, Dan and Tessa Logan have an ideal marriage—on the surface. But the pasts of both threaten their happiness, and send each into a tailspin. They do love each other, though, and learn that loving means forgiving even the deepest breaches of trust. I enjoyed seeing Dan and Tessa learn this, and I hope you do, too.

I love to hear from readers. E-mail me at kshay@rochester.rr.com or write to me at P.O. Box 24288, Rochester, NY 14624. And please visit my Web site at www.kathrynshay.com, and the Harlequin Superromance author site at www.superauthors.com.

Happy reading,

Kathryn Shay

TELL ME NO LIES
Kathryn Shay

TORONTO • NEW YORK • LONDON
AMSTERDAM • PARIS • SYDNEY • HAMBURG
STOCKHOLM • ATHENS • TOKYO • MILAN • MADRID
PRAGUE • WARSAW • BUDAPEST • AUCKLAND

EW

ISBN-13: 978-0-373-71359-2
ISBN-10: 0-373-71359-2

TELL ME NO LIES

This edition published by arrangement with Harlequin Books S.A.

® and TM are trademarks of the publisher. Trademarks indicated with ® are registered in the United States Patent and Trademark Office, the Canadian Trade Marks Office and in other countries.

www.eHarlequin.com

Printed in U.S.A.

Books by Kathryn Shay

HARLEQUIN SUPERROMANCE

For Zilla Soriano—
thanks for picking my first book out of the slush pile, loving
the rest of them and helping to make each better. I miss you.

CHAPTER ONE

As TESSA LOGAN POURED the jasmine bath salts into her claw-footed tub, she thought about her husband. Tonight they'd celebrate their tenth wedding anniversary. Picturing the evening to come, she smiled, turned on the taps and breathed in the scented steam. Her daughters were staying with her sister for the next twenty-four hours, and Dan would be home from work any time now. She hummed as she stood, pinned up her hair and undressed.

The dinner was ready. She'd placed a prime-rib roast in the oven, set the potatoes in the microwave to bake later, stuck the green salad she'd put together in the refrigerator and uncorked the merlot. The next sixty minutes were just for her.

She crossed into the bedroom, newly done in shades of green with white accents. Dan had been surprised at the redecoration, so different from the rest of the traditional colonial furniture and earth tones in the rest of their rambling Victorian. She didn't know why she'd taken this tack with the bedroom, except that once in a while she felt stifled by the constraints of her life.

The phone rang as she removed a box from her dresser drawer.

"Hello." She expected it to be Dan, and hoped he wasn't calling to say he'd be late getting home from work.

"Hey, Tessa." Her sister.

"Hi, Janey. Everything okay?"

"Yep. Just checking to make sure you're wearing the gift I bought for you."

"I've got it in my hand. I'm running my bath now." She chuckled. "You know Dan will be scandalized."

"St. Daniel could use some loosening up."

Tessa hesitated. "Don't tease about him, Janey. Please."

"Sorry." She could visualize her sister's hazel eyes, just like her own, filled with sympathy. Though they were six years apart, they seemed closer in age because they looked so much alike. "You know I love Dan to pieces. It's just that he's so straitlaced."

"Straitlaced is fine by me."

"But I hate to see you both missing some spice in your life."

"I promise, tonight there'll be plenty of spice. Are Sara and Molly having fun?"

"Are you kidding? My boys are falling all over them. They always wanted a sister. The four of them are out in the pool as we speak." She chuckled. "Of course, Molly's giving her cousins a run for their money, as usual. She's already hidden Jason's baseball glove and checked Jim's e-mail."

Tessa worried about her older child. Molly never got into real trouble, but she did enough damage to keep them all hopping. She seemed to take delight in shaking things up. "Put her on. I'll talk to her."

"No way. Go take your bath. Use scented oil," Janey added before she hung up.

A few minutes later Tessa climbed into the deep tub and sighed as she sank into the hot water. She lay back on the terry-cloth pillow, closed her eyes and listened to the Debussy CD she'd put on the stereo system in the bedroom. At one time she couldn't tell Debussy from Chopin. She hadn't known the difference between a van Gogh and a Picasso. When she'd become part of Dan's world, however, everything had changed.

Tessa pushed away her memories. She never let herself think about how she had lived before she met Dan because it was too painful. Tessa hadn't always been a good person. And her husband knew nothing about her past.

If Tessa had her way, he never would.

DAN LOGAN ENTERED the kitchen through the garage. He'd left work early, something he seldom did, but tonight was special, and he couldn't wait to get home. The girls were with Janey, and he and Tessa had the whole house to themselves. Stopping to put the red roses into a vase, he caught the scent of roasting meat and got a peek at the set table in the dining room. He smiled. The home Tessa had made for him was everything he wanted—well decorated, yet not ostentatious. A calm, peaceful haven after a day in the criminal world. Leaving her favorite flowers as a surprise for her when they came down to eat, he followed the sound of music up the back stairs.

He found his wife with her eyes closed, lounging in the tub. Glad to see she was pampering herself, he stood against the doorjamb of their bathroom and watched her. Her skin was flushed from the heat of the bath; her hair was piled on her head, with a few curls escaping around her face. She didn't take time for herself enough. She worked too hard, raising the girls and covering for him at home when his job as Orchard Place district attorney demanded late hours. She also worked part-time at the library and volunteered in the community.

"Hi, sweetheart."

She opened her eyes. Shades of brown and green, they warmed when they focused on him. "Hi." She lifted a leg covered with bubbles and glided a sponge-like thing over her calf. "I'm being lazy. I didn't expect you home so soon."

His gaze focused on the sensual gesture. Combined with the scent rising from the water, Dan was mesmerized. "I…was anxious to see you."

She directed a flirty smile at him. "Want to join me?"

His first impulse was to say yes. But then it surfaced, that rigid control he kept over every facet in his life. By now, it had become second nature. Tessa, however, could sometimes tempt him out of the self-imposed boundaries. Once in a while, in bed, he let her do that.

Covering the space between them, he bent over and kissed her cheek. "No, thanks. You know that tub's too small for me. I'm going to shower, though."

Back in the bedroom, he put his pocket change and his watch in the top drawer of the dresser, hung up his suit, placed his shoes on the second shelf at the bottom of the closet and stuffed his dirty clothes in the wicker laundry hamper. He smiled again at Tessa as he entered the bathroom and crossed to the shower in the corner.

She whistled at him. "Still looking good there, Dan."

"Nice to hear at forty," he said, stepping inside.

As he let the water sluice over him, he took pleasure in Tessa's compliment. Concentrating on the night ahead, he smiled as he washed. When he came out of the glass enclosure, Tessa had left her bath. Drying himself, shaving, he heard the music in the bedroom change to some Michael Bolton. The melody was romantic and…sexy. He felt his body respond. *Hmm.* Their habit was to make love at night, but what the hell, today was their anniversary.

Apparently, Tessa had the same thoughts, because when he entered the bedroom with a towel wrapped around his waist, she was on the bed.

"Where did you get that?"

She fingered the black lace strap of the top. "Janey bought it for me." Her hand slid to her thigh. "These, too," she said of the shorts-like panties to match.

The man in him, the husband and lover, responded to her tease. But then the staid person he'd become took over.

Tessa noticed. "You're frowning." Her eyes widened. "I'm sorry if this is too…risqué. I just thought…it's our anniversary."

The stricken look on her face—he'd seen it before and it always troubled him—sent him to the bed where he sat down next to her. "Shh," he said, kissing her tenderly. "It's not too risqué for your husband."

She didn't believe him.

"Tess, love, you know me. You know how conservative I am. I like it when you coax me out of that box."

"Do you?"

He touched the pearls around her neck. He'd given them to her on their wedding day, and he knew they'd become her most precious possession. "Of course." His grin was meant to soothe her. "You are so beautiful, and I love how this—" now he kissed the lacy edge of the top "—shows that off." He meant what he said, in his heart.

She relaxed. He ran his lips along the line of her collar bone and kissed his way over her body until all rational thought fled.

"WELL, I DON'T NEED to ask how your anniversary celebration was." Dan's brother Nick smirked at him with a cockiness left over from Nick's street days. "It's written all over your face."

Picking up his fork, Dan dug into his chicken Caesar salad. "Our anniversary was terrific. And it was nice to have time alone with Tessa. I'm crazy about my girls, but with Molly and Sara always there we don't have time to hold a decent conversation."

"Oh, yeah, I'll bet you talked all night long."

"None of your business, wise guy." Dan couldn't contain his smile. Last night had been full of fireworks. It stunned him that he could sometimes behave with such abandon.

"Yeah, yeah." Nick bit into his Reuben sandwich. "So what did you want to talk to me about?"

Dan's gaze was direct. "Mom."

Nick's hand curled around the glass in front of him. "Off limits, Dan. You know that."

"Her sixtieth birthday's next month. We're having a party, and I know she'd love it if you were there. If you'd give a little…"

"She kicked me out of the house when I was seventeen. I've done her a huge favor by avoiding contact since I came back. You aren't going to change that."

"She didn't kick you out. You left after she said you had to abide by her rules. I remember, Nick, I was there."

"Same thing. Anyway, Mom had you, the perfect child, in her house. I'm the disappointment."

"You're not a disappointment to me." Dan hoped his tone was as sincere as he felt. "You turned your life around."

"Yeah, I did."

The look on Nick's face told Dan his brother would close down if he didn't change the subject. "How's the job going?" His younger brother had come back to Orchard Place two years ago and now ran the town's Center for At-Risk Teens.

"The center's doing great, though we always need money and volunteers. Your wife's a big hit with the kids. The book discussion group she started at the library is thriving. I can't believe how well she relates to the girls."

"She works too hard. I worry about her."

"Mmm."

Dan's head came up. "Mmm, what?"

"I don't know. I worry about her, too, I guess."

Sipping his iced tea, Dan frowned.

"She ever talk about her past?" Nick asked.

"Why?"

"No reason. Does she?"

Since Tessa was circumspect about her background, he'd never discussed this with Nick before. "She grew up in the Midwest with Janey and a grandmother. No parents in the picture. She came east when…" He thought a minute. "I guess when her grandmother died. Anyway, she was a waitress in Chico's Diner and living with Janey when I met her."

"She seems sad to me sometimes."

Dan studied his brother, hating the fact that Nick might know information about Tessa he didn't. "Do you think something's wrong with her?"

"Nah." Nick set his napkin down on the table. "You, on the other hand, I could write a book about."

"Don't start." Dan concentrated on his salad.

"You live in fear that it's genetic, Dan."

The *it* didn't have to be clarified.

"I'm nothing like Dad was."

"I had his unethical tendencies in me."

"How did we get on to this topic?"

"Probably because you brought up Claire." Nick refused to call their mother Mom. "It's obvious that *she* thinks I got my bad seeds from him."

"That's crap."

"Then why have you spent your life in self-imposed perfection? I think you're trying to prove you're not like our embezzling bastard of a father."

"It's not necessary to get into this, Nick. I know I'm conservative because of our background. Tessa and I have discussed it. She accepts that about me. It works for us."

"Okay, fine."

"Let's talk about something else. How about your love life? Any women on the horizon?"

"Scores." Nick was always secretive about the women in his life, past and present.

"I'll bet that's true."

Nick had the Logan looks—dark hair and slate-blue eyes, classic bone structure. But whereas Nick held himself with easy grace and comfort, Dan was coiled up. Smiles came easily to Nick, while Dan was sober most of the time.

Well, he loved his brother and was grateful to have Nick back in his life. It was his father—the convicted felon—who Dan hated with a passion that wouldn't dissipate. Regardless of how much he talked to Tessa about it.

"Mom!" Nine-year-old Molly shouted the word from across the room, then hurtled herself at her mother as if Tessa had abandoned her for weeks, not left her one day with her favorite cousins. "I *missed* you." Molly's grin was infectious, and she always made Tessa smile. Her carefree child loved life and showed it with exuberant charm.

"I missed you, too, Mol." Tessa hugged her and glanced over at Janey, who was rolling her eyes. "Well, I did."

"Did you and Dad have a good time on your anniversary?"

"Yeah, *did* you have a good time?" Janey teased.

Tessa drew back. "We did."

"What'd ya do, Mom?"

"Oh, grown-up stuff."

Very grown-up stuff. She shivered at the thought of how Dan had touched her last night. She loved it when he lost himself in their lovemaking. It didn't happen every time, but she treasured those rare occasions he couldn't even remember his name.

"Hi, Mom." Sara stood in the doorway. At almost eight, fourteen months younger than Molly, she eyed Tessa warily. She looked like her dad with dark hair and blue eyes, whereas Molly had inherited Tessa's hazel eyes and light brown hair. Molly's hair fell in curls down her back, but these days Tessa blew her hair straight.

"Hey, baby. Come give me a hug."

Sara approached her with dainty little steps. She hugged Tessa tentatively. Her younger daughter was quiet and self-contained. Again, like her dad.

"Go pack up your stuff, now. We have to do some grocery shopping before dinner."

"Can we get ice cream?" Molly asked. "The kind Aunt Janey has, with pieces of candy bars in it?"

"I think so. Just as long as you don't overdo it."

When the girls were gone, Janey sat at her kitchen table and Tessa followed suit. "Sara's too serious,"

Janey said. "It would be healthy for her to overdo it once in a while."

"Maybe."

"You, too."

Tessa's sister had a strong protective streak, evident all through their youth, and when Tessa came to live with her in Orchard Place. Even now that they were adults with their own families, she played mother hen frequently.

"You know why I'm like this."

"The accident wasn't your fault." Janey hesitated before she continued. "That anniversary is coming up, too."

"Please, don't talk about it. I can't risk somebody finding out."

Janey's expression turned sad. "You should tell Dan."

"After his father's situation? Are you kidding? We'd never have gotten together if he'd known about me."

"Hey, he was the one who pursued you. Relentlessly, I might add."

That was true. Though she'd fallen hook, line and sinker for the young Orchard County assistant district attorney, it took him six months to wheedle a date out of her, a year until she slept with him. She wouldn't have married him but she'd gotten pregnant, which a few weeks later ended in miscarriage.

"It doesn't matter what happened in the past,

Janey. With Grandma dead, you're the only one who knows the truth. Not telling Dan is a done deal."

"I'm not the only one who knows the truth. That lunatic—"

Tessa felt her face pale. "Janey, no. Don't even say his name. Please. We made a pact."

"All right, all right. I won't even say his name. I hope he's burning in hell, anyway."

KANSAS FEDERAL Penitentiary had become Frankie Hamilton's own personal hell. He stared out his cell window at the barbed wire fences and dirty, white guard tower, his hate for the place burning inside him. He'd been down for fifteen years and only the black-market buck, which got him drunk, kept him from going postal all this time.

"Hey, Hamilton, you over there?"

Coughing from the freakin' dampness of the prison—he swore he'd had this cold for years—Frankie dragged himself to the front of the cell and plunked down on the end of his cot. The flimsy bed, a cheap steel desk and chair, a sink and a toilet furnished the concrete ten-by-ten room. It smelled like piss and cleanser. "Yeah, Shank, I'm here. Where you think I am, at a ball?"

"Just checking. I hate Sunday nights in this place."

"Why they any worse than the rest of the week?"

"My pa never came home on Sunday nights. Me and my ma—it was the only peace we had."

It had been rumored among the inmates that Sammy Shanker, aka Shank, had blown off the back of his father's head one cold winter morning and splattered his old man's brains all over his own face. He'd been seventeen at the time.

"You get any more letters from your ma?"

"Not this week. Maybe tomorrow." Shank swore. "You heard from your girl?"

Frankie glanced to the desk and grinned. "Another letter yesterday."

"Read me some? 'Cause it's Sunday?"

"I dunno."

"Not the private parts."

Frankie rose from the cot, grabbed the sealed envelope off the desk and came back to the front of the cell. He put the letter to his nose; he knew it had a flowery scent but he couldn't smell it because he was constantly stuffed up. "Maybe a little bit." He tore open the envelope and smiled at the familiar handwriting.

"Dear Frankie, I miss you so much. I can't wait till you get out on parole in a few weeks. I'm sending another picture so you don't forget me."

"Can I see it?"

"Sure." Snaking his arm between the bars and out as far as he could, he let Shank get a peek at his girl.

"She don't look much different than the last picture."

Frankie snatched his hand back; his head started to hurt. "Course she does." He rubbed his thumb and finger over his eyes, then stared at the curly, light brown hair, the wide brown eyes, the freckles on her nose.

"Frankie? Read some more?"

When the pain receded, he read parts of the three pages. The end of the letters always made him feel better. "I love you, Frankie, and can't wait till you get out. Come back to me soon. Love, Trixie."

Trixie, his girl. Frankie lay back on his bed, remembering her baby-soft skin and silky hair. He'd never forgive the damned prison system for splitting them up. She'd been sentenced to a different jail all those years ago and had gone back to the real world after eighteen months. Kissing the picture, he whispered, "It won't be long now, Trixie."

Frankie fell asleep with Trixie next to his heart.

CHAPTER TWO

THE SMELL OF FRESH FLOWERS filtered in through the open windows of Tessa's dark green SUV. The beginning of May in western New York was breathtaking. Tessa, who also liked the wintertime snow, couldn't understand why people would reside anywhere else. Living in a town with a population of twenty thousand, Tessa had to drive to most places, but although she hated being behind the wheel of a car, she was used to it. Today, she was heading toward the girls' school. Molly had a doctor's appointment and Tessa didn't have to work until the afternoon.

She passed Carlson's Drugs, reminding herself to drop by later with Dan's prescription. She frowned. His blood pressure was up again. She tried to banish the worry that continued to niggle at her. Nothing was going to happen to him. The condition would soon be under control.

The stoplight changed and, putting her foot on the gas, she started out into the intersection. A fleeting glimpse of red registered before she felt the impact. There was a loud crack, like a bat hitting a ball. The passenger side crumpled. The car spun out into the other lane of traffic.

She gripped the wheel. *How should I turn it? What am I supposed to do?* Her SUV slammed into a tree, then for a moment all was eerily still.

Finally she heard someone yell, "Call 911!"

A man yelled to her through her window. Tessa tried to look at him, to tell him she was okay, but when she moved, pain exploded in her forehead, radiating everywhere. She closed her eyes.

Sirens.

When she opened her eyes again, a red truck was in her line of vision.

"Ma'am? Are you all right?"

She tried to speak, but she couldn't.

"Get the ram over here, the door's stuck!"

The voices began to fade and the shouts came from farther away now. Dizziness engulfed her. She thought she might throw up.

Everything went black.

A loud pop startled her awake. The door to the SUV was ripped off.

"Ma'am. I'm Lieutenant Jacobs. I…holy hell, Tessa? I didn't recognize your car. It's me, Jake, from three doors down."

Only a squeak came out of her mouth when Tessa tried to answer.

Jake turned and said to somebody, "Get me a collar and the backboard." She felt a soothing hand on her head. "Don't worry, Tessa, we'll get you out of here."

Before she faded back into unconsciousness, she heard, "Call Dan Logan at the DA's office. Tell him to get to the hospital right away."

COLD FEAR LODGED in his throat as Dan rushed into emergency ten minutes after his assistant found him about to begin the trial.

Please, God, please, let her be all right.

He found Janey in the waiting room, huddled in a chair, her face ashen. As he got closer, he saw her hands twisting a handkerchief.

"Oh, no, Janey, what—?"

"She's all right. Brad saw her before her own doctor came in. He said she's got bruises and she's shaken, but it doesn't look like there's any serious damage." Janey drew in a breath. "Her doctor told Brad to tell us to wait out here and she'd find us after she examined Tessa." Thank God Janey's husband was a doctor.

His body went limp. Closing his eyes, he forced himself to calm down. Dan could do this now. He could do anything so long as she was all right. "What happened?"

Janey looked over his shoulder.

Dan tracked her gaze and saw a firefighter coming toward him.

"Hey, Dan," Jake, their neighbour, said. "I was the first responder. Tessa's rattled and bruised, but basically fine."

"You're sure?"

"Her doctor's examining her, but, yeah, I think she's okay. Except…"

"Except what?"

"She's really shaken. We had to pry her hands off the steering wheel. They're black and blue from holding it so tight."

"Is that uncommon in a car accident?"

"It happens. But she also kept saying she was sorry."

"Poor Tessa." She hated to drive and this would make it worse. "Was she at fault?"

"Nope. A red Mustang T-boned her when he ran a light. Luckily on the passenger side, which was empty."

His stomach roiled. If one of the girls had been with her…

"The driver of the Mustang is okay, too. He admitted the accident was his fault."

"It's just like Tessa to believe she could have driven more defensively so this didn't have to happen," Janey said.

"She's a sweetheart." Jake smiled. "My kids love her. Anyway, count your blessings it wasn't any worse."

When Jake left, Dan turned to Janey. "I think it's more than what you said."

"What do you mean?"

"Tessa hates to drive. She didn't even have her license when I met her, which is odd for someone her age."

Her sister said nothing.

"Look, Janey, you know that accident when she was nineteen made her gun-shy. I had to coax her into learning to drive after we were married."

Janey sank into a chair. "That would make anybody gun-shy, wouldn't it?"

Dan dropped into an adjacent seat. "I guess." He watched Janey fidget with her wedding ring, and his gut instinct—the one that made him a successful lawyer—kicked in. "Is there something I should know?"

"No, nothing."

He grasped Janey's hand. It was cold and clammy. "Honey, I'm crazy about your sister. If there's any way I can help her, please tell me."

"What do you want to know?"

"What was she like when she had the accident? I know so little about how you two grew up. I wish I had more information, but it upsets Tessa to talk about it."

"You know the important details."

Some of them, he thought. They never knew their father. Their mother drank and took off with some guy when they were little. Child protective let them live with their grandmother.

"Tessa said she worked in a diner after high school. I always wondered why she didn't go to college. She did great at Buffalo University when she got her librarian's degree."

"Sometimes people aren't ready for college right away."

"That's what she said." But he always thought she was hedging. Just like Janey was doing right now.

"You've been so good for her, Dan. That's all that counts."

"Dan, is that you?"

He glanced up to see that their doctor, Lisa Benton, had come out of E.R. "How is she, Lisa?"

"Physically, she's fine. Emotionally, she's shaken."

"Pretty common after an accident, right?" This from Janey.

"Yes, often it is." Lisa looped her stethoscope around her neck and looked down at a chart. "But Tessa's response is a bit exaggerated. She's quiet and withdrawn. She'll answer my questions, but there's some kind of, I don't know, fear in her behavior."

"She hates driving," Dan said.

"Maybe that's all it is."

"Should we do anything?" Janey asked.

"Not now. Take her home, keep her in bed the rest of the day, and call me tomorrow. If she's still this upset, we'll think about what to do."

"All right."

"I can stay with her," Janey said after the doctor left.

Dan looked askance. "I'm not going back to work after this."

"Okay. Could I have some time alone with her?"

An odd request. "Why?"

Janey's lower lip trembled. "I was scared that something bad was going to happen to her, Dan."

Janey loved Tessa unconditionally. And he knew being with Janey was good for his wife. Her mood was lighter after her visits with her sister or even after talking to Janey on the phone.

Dan touched her shoulder. "Tell you what. We'll get her home and make sure she's all right. The girls will need to see her, then I'll take them to a McDonald's restaurant and you can have an hour alone with her."

"Thanks, Dan. For understanding our bond."

"Janey, I want what's best for Tessa. If being with you for a while will help, so be it." He put his arm around her. "Now let's go get our girl."

Tessa burst into tears when Dan walked through the curtains of her cubicle in the E.R.

He strode to the bed. "Oh, sweetheart, I'm so sorry."

"It was my fault," she said, clinging to him, burying her face in his chest. This was what she needed now. His closeness. The feel and scent of him. "I should have been more careful. I should have waited at the light longer."

His hand in her hair was soothing. He kissed the top of her head. "Tess, the driver of the other car admitted guilt. He said he ran the signal light. He took legal responsibility. None of this was your fault."

"It's all my fault."

"No, no."

After a moment, his steady heartbeat quieted her and she drew back. She raised her hands to her cheeks and flinched. "My face hurts."

"It's banged up a little."

Her gaze flew to Janey.

"The bruises will go away," Janey said.

On the outside, maybe. Tessa fell back into the pillow. "Lisa said I can go home, right?"

"Uh-huh. As soon as you get dressed and I sign the papers."

She took Dan's hand. It was big, and holding it always made her feel safe. But she had to be careful here. "I'm okay. Just shaken. When I think that Molly and Sara could have been with me. The other car hit the passenger side so hard."

Dan drew a handkerchief out of his pocket, and she wiped her eyes. "They weren't with you. They're safe with my mother. She picked them up after school and brought them to her condo."

"Do they know what happened?"

"Not yet. I wanted to wait to tell them until they could see you in person.

"I'll stay with you while he gets the girls," Janey said.

"Oh, okay."

Dan kissed her nose. "I'm so sorry you have to go through this, honey. I know driving is hard for you. This must be your worst nightmare."

"I'll be fine." She fisted her hands in the lapels of his suit coat. "I'm sorry I'm being such a baby."

"You're entitled." He stood. "Want me to help you get dressed?"

"I'll do it." Janey stepped closer to the bed. "Maybe you can take care of the hospital stuff."

Dan cocked his head and looked puzzled. "Sure." He squeezed Tessa's shoulder, and walked out of the cubicle.

When Dan was gone, Janey sat down on the side of the bed and enfolded Tessa in her arms. "Oh, God, Janey, what did I do?"

"You did nothing. Not this time or the last."

"Yes, yes I did."

She could still hear the screeching tires and breaking glass. The screams and the sirens.

"Don't associate the two accidents, honey. They're unrelated."

"I was driving this time."

"I know."

"I couldn't live with myself if I hurt someone again."

"The only person hurt today was you."

Releasing her sister, Tessa lay back. When she

closed her eyes, she could feel the terror creep up on her. "I can't forget what happened fifteen years ago. This has brought it all back in Technicolor vividness."

Before Tessa could say anything, the curtain swung back. Dan stood in the entryway.

How much had he heard?

"DOES IT HURT, MOMMY?" Molly cuddled into Tessa on their bed, and Dan watched his wife wince. Sara stood across the room in the safe circle of his arm.

"Yes, sweetie, a little bit."

"Hey, kiddo," Dan said to Molly, "I think your snuggling could be a little less fervent today."

Molly glanced over at him. If it had been Sara, Dan wouldn't have said anything and let Tessa bear the brunt of her daughter's enthusiasm. Sara was sensitive and unsure of herself and even a gentle chiding would have made her feel bad.

But Molly was tough. Maybe too tough. "Okay, Daddy." She drew back, and touched the purple bruises on Tessa's face. "It looks yucky."

"I know, Mol. But what's most important is that nobody was hurt."

Not today, anyway.

Dan had overheard his wife and Janey talking in the E.R. Once again, he squelched his anxiety that Tessa was keeping something from him. Something important. He'd have to deal with that sooner or later, and he would, but Tessa was at her worst right now and he wasn't going to force the issue.

Even if secrets were abhorrent to him. Even after he'd made Tessa promise she wouldn't lie to him, either outright or by omission, as his parents had. She was the one person he'd trusted in his life to be honest with him.

He made sure there was no concern in his voice when he said to the girls, "Are you two ready to eat yet?"

Molly catapulted off the bed. "McDonald's!" she shouted. "They got a mad-cool slide in the playground now."

Sara buried her face in his waist. "I don't want to leave Mom."

"How about if you visit alone with Mom for a few minutes, then you come with us."

"Okay." Letting go of him, Sara crept to the bed and perched on the side.

Molly skipped over to Dan. "Come on, Dad."

"We'll go keep Aunt Janey company. Sara, five minutes."

His little girl nodded. As he left the room hand in hand with Molly, he saw Tessa wince again as Sara, albeit gently, went into her mother's open embrace.

Janey was fixing iced tea when they came down to the kitchen. "All ready to go?" she asked Dan.

The roses sat on the table, reminding him that it had been their anniversary only a few days ago. Everything had been fine then. Now, his wife was bruised as a boxer, and he'd discovered there was something more to that accident in her past that he didn't know about.

Molly snitched a cookie from the jar and said, "I'm goin' outside to wait for you and slowpoke."

"Go ahead, Mol."

When she left, Dan watched Janey fuss with a tray filled with tea and crackers, which was all Tessa wanted to eat. Though Janey wasn't any bigger or heavier than her sister, she always seemed sturdy and strong, whereas Tessa appeared fragile.

"Why are you staring at me like that?"

He folded his arms over his chest. "I overheard you two in the hospital when you thought you were alone."

If he wasn't sure before that something was going on, he was now. Janey went pale.

"Don't bother to deny it. I heard you talking about what happened fifteen years ago. I assume it was the accident that caused Tessa to hate to drive. The one you and I discussed."

"Dan, I—"

He held up his hand. "No, I'm not asking you to betray a confidence. As soon as she's better, I'll get it all out in the open myself. Now, she's too raw."

"All right."

"I love your sister." He gave her a smile because she looked so sad. "Almost as much as you do."

Janey's return smile was weak.

"Now take the roses upstairs, too, so Tessa can enjoy them. And send my other daughter down."

As she walked by him holding the tray, Janey stopped and kissed his cheek.

He placed a hand on her shoulder. "Don't worry. I won't upset her now."

"Thanks, Dan."

When Sara joined him a few minutes later and they went out to find Molly, Dan put his cause for concern out of his mind. Since he'd become an expert at repressing negative thoughts, he was able, for the time being, to forget this one.

"So, Frankie, your walkaway day's coming up next week."

Frankie was sitting at a table in the cafeteria with Shank, sipping hot tea that tasted awful. But he'd been to the infirmary again for this damned cold, and they told him warm liquids would help. The consistently loud din in this place hurt his ears and the bright lighting made him squint. "Yep, it is."

"How's it feel to be getting out?"

"Feels right, Shank."

"I'm gonna miss you."

"Me, too." That was a lie. Frankie couldn't wait to be done with this place. He couldn't wait to see Trixie again.

"She coming to get you?"

Shank had some crazy obsession where Trixie

was concerned. If they were on the outside, he'd beat the crap out of any guy for thinking about her that much. Frankie was a jealous man—and proud of it. Trixie was his, and if any other guy got near her, he'd bust the jerk's face open.

"Is she coming for you, Frank?"

"Um, no. She can't get off… She isn't… I'm gonna surprise her." His vision blurred some. He blinked hard to clear it. "She don't know the exact date."

But he did. He'd been counting the days. It was fifteen years ago today since the stupid accident and only a week more on his sentence. During the trial, the judge had had it in for Frankie and was jonesing to put him away. In the end, they separated Frankie from Trixie because everybody hated him. But she didn't and that's all that counted now. He'd see her soon.

In a line of prisoners, he left the cafeteria. A guard at the front took a group of them and veered off to the library. Since he was about to be paroled, they'd started letting him use the Internet. He got right online after the assistant read him the dumb-ass rules again; he clicked into his hometown Web site, Iverton, Ohio. *The Iverton Banner* was posted every day.

Same old, same old. New superintendent of schools. An issue up before the city council on paving the streets. Minor break-ins and petty larceny on the police page.

He stopped short at the headline on section B.

Fifteen Year Anniversary of Tragic Accident. Shit, small towns. They never forgot nothing. You couldn't make one single mistake without it following you for life. He was going back there to get Trixie, but he planned to leave that hick town in the dust. Morbid curiosity made him read the article.

Fifteen years ago today, Franklin R. Hamilton ran a red light and drove his car into the back end of a Chevy truck, killing Mrs. Serena Summers and her daughter, Joanna, age five. Shock filled our small community when it was discovered that both Hamilton and his companion, Tessa Lawrence, had been smoking marijuana and drinking alcohol. An undisclosed amount of cocaine was also found in the trunk of the car.

Frankie stopped reading. Tessa? Who was she? For a minute he didn't remember. Then he did—her sister called her that. Frankie had given her a nickname. To him, she was always Trixie. His Trixie.

Hamilton was sentenced to twenty years in a federal penitentiary for negligent homicide and possession of a controlled substance, and Lawrence received three years in a federal prison camp on the possession charge. Lawrence was released on probation after serving eighteen months. Hamilton is up for parole as this article is being written. He refused to talk to reporters at the prison. The husband and father of the slain family could not be reached for comment.

The reporter then went on to enumerate statistics about drunk drivers and increased penalties for DUI and drug possession, and ended with a comment about never being able to make up for such an atrocity.

Screw them, Frankie logged off the Web site. His life was gonna be just fine, as soon as he could get out of here and be with Trixie again.

Hmm. It was time for another letter from her.

CHAPTER THREE

DAN WANTED A CONVICTION on Eddie Cramden in the worst way. As the defendant sat in the witness chair, wearing a spiffy suit his rich father had most likely bought him and his hair slicked back in a ponytail, Dan had to curb the vehement urge to nail the guy. He forced himself to wait until his assistant district attorney brought in the new evidence that had come to light last night.

Cramden was on trial for a VOP, violation of probation, and Dan was losing his case. The witness who was to testify that Cramden had completed a drug transaction had recanted, so Cramden was off the hook not only for that crime, but for the VOP, which had been hinging on the drug deal. For his entire career in the D.A.'s office, Dan had fought to get drug dealers and users off the street and away from innocents, like his family.

The judge sat behind her oak bench, her face inscrutable, and nodded to him. "Mr. Logan, would you like to cross-examine the witness?"

In his peripheral vision, Dan saw Karen Jackson, his assistant D.A., enter the courtroom carrying a folder and, better yet, smiling.

"Yes, Your Honor, I would. Might I have a minute to confer with my colleague?"

"Do you want a recess?"

"I don't think so. I need to confirm the relevance of a question I have for Mr. Cramden."

In her no-nonsense way, Karen handed him the folder. "Got it. K-Mart store, last year. The amount was low, so he pleaded guilty to a noncriminal offense of disorderly conduct when he appeared before a judge at the arraignment. Though at that time he was indeed on probation, he was never prosecuted, therefore no one got him on the VOP. His daddy managed to make the charge go away."

"*Hoo*ray." Dan strode to the witness stand and stood in front of Cramden. The guy was at ease because he'd been informed before the proceedings got under way that Dan had no case. Which had been true up until a few minutes ago. "Mr. Cramden, were you ever arrested for shoplifting?"

"Objection!" Allison Markham, the defense attorney, was on her feet. A partner in a prestigious firm, she was one of the best criminal lawyers in town. "Mr. Cramden is not on trial for shoplifting."

"Mr. Logan, are you going somewhere with this?" Judge Wicker asked.

"Yes, Your Honor."

Sweat began to bead on Cramden's face, and he frowned over at his father, who was paying Allison's enormous fees. "I didn't get a conviction for shoplifting."

Dan held up the file. "I have here a document that shows you were involved in an incident at a K-Mart store."

Cramden's smiled disappeared. "That was nothing. I didn't get charged with a crime."

"Approach, Your Honor." In her blue power suit, Allison was already marching to the bench. "What's going on, Dan?"

"Your client was picked up at a local discount store for shoplifting. He stole a ten-dollar fishing pole."

"Was he arrested?" the judge asked.

"No, he got off with noncriminal disorderly conduct." He nodded back to the rows of spectator seats where the indulgent father sat. "A deal was made."

Judge Wicker's eyes narrowed on Dan. "You know, Mr. Logan, any case involving prosecution for ten dollars is liable to be thrown out of court."

"Maybe not. Given the security tape and the testimony of the supervisor we just obtained, which wasn't used before, a judge might reconsider opening the case. If he does, even *prosecution* for the incident constitutes a violation of probation."

Though a judge might *not* consider opening the case, the defense couldn't afford to take the chance that Cramden would go back to jail for ten years.

Allison's face flamed. "I know nothing about this! The D.A. withheld evidence."

"That came to us only minutes ago."

"This is a witch hunt."

Judge Wicker bristled. "Violation of probation, no matter how minute, is something my court takes seriously, Ms. Markham. I'm adjourning for today in hopes you and Mr. Logan can come to some agreement so we don't have to go through a full-fledged trial."

Stifling a grin, Dan knew he had the guy.

Allison came to the same conclusion. By four, they had a plea bargain and Cramden was headed back to prison for three years. Happy, Dan sauntered to his office. He was meeting Tessa at the library at five and they were going to the lake for dinner. Nick was taking the girls to SeaBreeze, a local amusement park.

Dan dropped down behind his desk. *Tessa.* Now that he had a minute to think, he played back what had happened in the week since her car accident. Most of the bruises on her face had faded, but the ones on her legs and butt were still nasty. Poor baby. Her mood had improved, too, and she was no longer blaming herself for the crash. He'd waited until last night to bring up the question he'd had about her past....

"Tess, honey, sit with me a minute."

She'd been standing at the kitchen counter, and he had taken a chair at the table. "I should finish up the salad."

"In a minute. The kids are watching a video. I'd like to talk to you about something."

She had sat down. "What's going on?"

"When you were in the emergency room, I overheard you and Janey talking about the car accident you had when you were nineteen. You said something about still feeling guilty."

Her hands had clenched the skirt she wore. "Did I? I don't remember."

"Tess, love, you can tell me anything. We all make mistakes."

There had been a wounded look in her eyes. "I didn't have a happy childhood, and I had a worse adolescence." She had drawn in a breath. "One of the reasons I didn't want a relationship with you all those years ago was because you were always prying into my past. I hate it when you do this."

The accusation had stung. Sure, Tessa had been more than wary of his attention when she worked at Chico's Diner and waited on him. She refused—innumerable times—to date him. He didn't remember one of the reasons being his interest in her past, though.

"No, I haven't forgotten what happened eleven years ago. Or the fact that you only agreed to marry me because you were pregnant."

Her face had shadowed at the reminder of the baby she'd lost.

"Dan, why are we going over all this? You know

I love you, the kids and our life together. What possible reason could there be for you to delve into something so painful for me?"

"The car accident made you sad."

"Right now, *you're* making me sad."

So he'd dropped it....

Tonight he hoped to make up to her for being so pushy. He should have let it go, he guessed. Sometimes, his overprotectiveness caused him to be too aggressive. Maybe he'd leave work early and pick up some flowers for her.

He was stuffing things into his briefcase when the administrative assistant, Wanda Anderson, strode into the office. "Dan, Mayor Nash is here to see you."

"Why?"

Wanda shrugged. "He's with two city councilmen. They said they want to talk to you right away."

This was unusual. He circled his desk and went to the door to greet them, hoping this wasn't bad news, hoping he got out of this meeting in time to meet his wife.

"THAT'S A WISE CHOICE, Chelsea. It's one of my favorites in the series."

Book in hand, the pretty blonde with world-weary blue eyes looked over at Tessa. "I already read *Go Ask Alice* and *Jay's Journal.*"

Tessa nodded to the book. "*Annie's Baby* is as

well written as those." She held the girl's gaze. "Want to talk about anything, sweetie?"

Chelsea Chamberlain shrugged with typical teenage nonchalance. "Talk about what?"

Tessa had been working with this particular group of girls from Nick's center every Thursday since September, and had gotten close to them. In the last few weeks, she'd begun to suspect Chelsea was pregnant. Tessa wondered how much to say. Kids hated to be pushed. *She* hated to be pushed. Something Dan did routinely, as he'd shown last night.

Before Tessa could respond, another teen, Jill, came up to them. Dark-eyed and intense, she said, "Hunk alert."

Tessa laughed. She'd gotten used to the girls drooling over her brother-in-law. Nick was the center's school liaison and focused on keeping troubled kids in classes, steering them away from drugs and into healthier endeavors, helping them keep their grades up. Dan, who'd had contact with Nick over the years, had been shocked to find out that he'd earned a degree in counseling in Rockford. "Is Nick here already?"

"Yeah." Jill sighed. "He wants to see you when you're done steering us to lesson-laden literature."

"Great alliteration." She cocked her head. "Do you mind so much? I thought reading about teenagers your age might help you figure things out."

"You're such an easy mark, Mrs. L. We're cool.

We like it better than those classics you had us reading when we first came here. Except maybe that doll's house play, where the chick finally blows off her deadbeat husband."

Tessa left them and found Nick staring at a glass-enclosed case full of books. From a distance, she could admire the long lines of his build, his dark hair and his almost navy eyes. In some ways he looked like his brother, and in some ways they could be complete strangers.

"Hey, how's my favorite brother-in-law?"

Nick winked at her. "I'll bet you say that to Brad, too."

"That's right. I'm an equal opportunity sister-in-law."

"How are you feeling today?"

Nodding to the stacks where the girls had been drooling over him, she said, "I'm well enough to do this. I'm coming back to work here tomorrow."

"Bruises look better."

Self-consciously, she touched her face. "Finally!"

"How are my girls doing?"

"They're on to me." She told him about Jill's remark.

Nick laughed. "You're pretty transparent. I think that's why they like you. What you see is what you get."

She had to clear her throat. "I like them, too."

"I'm ready to take them back, then go pick up my nieces at their friend's house."

"Thanks for watching them tonight."

"Dan said he wanted an evening alone with you." He squeezed her shoulder. "I think you scared him half to death with that accident. Me, too."

"Still, you have better things to do than babysit."

"I have nothing better to do than spend time with my two nieces." He glanced at his watch. "You can return the favor, though."

"Anything."

"The guys at the center are jealous of this little Thursday excursion the girls get to take. They want equal time. Could you manage that somehow in your schedule? They could come to the library when you're working your part-time shifts."

She hesitated only a split second, but Nick must have caught it. Sometimes, he was too good at reading people.

"You don't like working with the boys, do you?"

"I prefer to be with the girls." The boys reminded her too much of someone else, long ago.

"Forget it then. I can do something else with them that they'll like as much."

"No, no, I want to help out. You never ask me anything."

"Tessa, really, it's okay."

Dan came bursting through the front door of the library, precluding any further discussion. His face was lit with excitement. Anticipation. She knew him so well, had studied his moods, so she could prepare for them.

He placed a hand on her shoulder. "Hello, sweetheart."

"Hi."

"You look like you could scale Mt. Everest," Nick said. "Did something happen?"

"Yeah. I'm glad you're both here." He grinned at his brother. "And that I have Tessa alone tonight. We've got something to celebrate."

"What?" Tessa asked, already smiling.

"I'm being named Citizen of the Year."

"Oh, Dan, that's terrific." The award had been instituted two years ago, and Tessa was hoping it would fall his way.

"Yeah, terrific." Nick tried to sound enthusiastic, but Dan's need for respectability always grated on him.

"Come on, Nick. It's my thing, even if it isn't yours. There's a banquet honoring me next month. I want everybody there."

Tessa had caught his excitement. "The girls, Janey and her family…"

"And our mother, right?" Nick asked.

"Of course." Dan said.

"I'll let you know." Nick clapped Dan on the shoulder. "Congrats, Dan. I'm happy for you." He started to walk away. "I have to find the kids."

"Nicky?" Tessa called out.

"Yes?"

"Will you come to the award dinner?"

"Sure."

After he left, Dan said, "He won't. Not if Mom's there."

"Oh, dear."

"Don't." In a rare display of public affection, he picked her up and twirled her around. "No negative thoughts. Nothing's going to spoil this for me. Nothing."

JACKHAMMERS WERE GOING OFF in his head. He sneezed into his handkerchief, then blew his nose. Frankie was ready to smash somebody's face in as he rode the Iverton bus to the outskirts of town. Trixie wasn't here. How could she not be here?

He'd scoured the place for her. First, he'd gone to her grandmother's house. The shingles were new and the porch refurbished, and somebody else owned the place. Grandma Addie was gone. No loss there. She'd hated him….

Get out of here, you're not welcome.

Trixie says I am.

You're not right in the head. Leave her alone.

And when they'd gotten in trouble she'd screamed at him again. *You crazy bastard. You corrupted her. She was a good girl until you came along.*

He'd told the old biddy to go to hell. Trixie was his, and he could do anything he wanted with her. Hadn't she told him that, in the letters stuffed in his duffel bag?

The ugly industrial scenery of downtown Iverton rolled by. He'd checked out the diner where she had worked all those years ago. They had new owners, too, who didn't remember any Trixie Lawrence.

Now, he was headed to the south side of town. That bitch Janey, who was always trying to interfere, always trying to protect Trixie from *him*, for God's sake, had ditched this place, too. But her old boyfriend, Teaker, still lived here. He might know something about Trixie.

Frankie got off at Farrell Street and walked up the hill; the bartender at Crane's Beer Hall had told him where Teaker lived. *Man, what a dump*, Frankie thought as he found the shack. An old man tottered out.

"I'm lookin' for Teaker. The guy at Crane's says he lived here."

The man came closer. "I'm Teaker. Who are… holy shit, Frankie, is that you?"

Frankie knew his mouth dropped. "What happened to you?"

"Fifteen years, Frank. You look older, too."

Can't be as bad as you. He ran his fingers through his gray hair, noticed the veins in his other hand were more pronounced. "I guess."

"I had some bad times. Not as bad as you, though. I never went down. How'd ya hold up in there?"

"Letters. From Trixie."

"I thought she was in the can, too."

"Got out after a while. She wrote me every day from here. That's why I'm back."

"Trixie? She ain't living in Iverton no more."

"I don't get it." Frankie cocked his head and thought hard. The pain, which had started to recede, instantly came back. "Got any beer?"

"Yeah, sure. Come onto the porch."

Frankie sat on a rickety chair under an overhang. Once he chugged some ale, he could think more clearly. "You ever hear from Janey?"

"Shit, no. She married some doctor and went to live in New York."

His heart began to beat fast. "New York's a big place. The city?"

Teaker lit a cigar and sat back. "Nah. On a lake, I think."

"There's a shitload of lakes in New York."

"I dunno which one."

"Who might?"

His old drinking buddy raised his bushy gray eyebrows. "I think there was somethin' in the paper a while back about her doctor husband getting a grant to find a cure for some disease."

"Yeah? Who'd know about that?"

"Maybe Mrs. Fox."

Frankie recognized the name of the librarian he and his buddies used to terrorize. "Hell, she ain't dead yet?"

"She's too mean to die, Frankie."

"You remember Janey's new name?"

"Nope. But the article could tell you."

Frankie finished his beer and crumpled the can in

his fist. Promising to bring up a six-pack later that night and reminisce about old times, he left.

No way was he going to come back, though. He wouldn't waste his time with *that* loser when he could be looking for Trixie. Frankie still couldn't figure out all those letters coming from Iverton, if she hadn't been here.

He found old lady Fox at the library. She was ancient now and just as nasty. Everybody in this hick town treated him like dirt. Everybody was always after him. The bitch turned him over to her younger staff member, who found the article on the computer for him.

He read it anxiously.

Janey Lawrence…Christopher.

Married the up-and-coming doctor, had two boys.

Bingo! In Orchard Place, New York.

Almost as an afterthought, he googled the husband. The guy had a freakin' Web site for his practice and the grant thing Teaker told him about. It also had a section on family. He clicked that link. There was Janey. Older, heavier, but Janey all the same. She had Trixie's looks, but Trixie was prettier. He waded through photos of the kids, the colleagues. The last picture was a family shot of all the Christophers. And arm in arm with Janey was her sister. Tessa. God he hated when people called her that. He stared at the different hair and clothes, but she had the same eyes, mouth and features of his beloved Trixie. He'd recognize that face anywhere. Glancing around, he printed off the picture.

Frankie smiled all the way to the bus station. If Janey was in Orchard Place, chances were her sister would be there. Those two were like Siamese twins. And Janey had hated Frankie with a passion. She'd tried every way she could to break them up but never could.

At the bus station, he bought his ticket. The attendant told him it was a ten-hour ride from Iverton to Orchard Place, stopping several times. But Frankie didn't care. He was gonna see Trixie. He might have to bitch-slap her around some for not staying put, but after that there'd be pure bliss.

Finally, him and Trixie were going to be together again.

CHAPTER FOUR

TESSA ARRANGED FOOD at the picnic table on the patio of her sister's home, where the family had gathered for their Memorial Day picnic. The sun was shining and the sky was cloudless; a warm breeze wafted over her, carrying the sweet sound of chirping birds, making this a halcyon afternoon.

"I like seeing that."

Tessa looked up at Janey's husband, Brad, who'd come over from the grill. "What do you like seeing?"

"You smiling." He slid his arm around her. "We were worried after the accident. Your sister freaked."

"I'm sorry she spends her time fretting over me. She always has, Brad. I can't seem to break her of the habit."

Brad shook his head—he was mostly bald now and had shaved off what was left of his hair. Still, he was fit and youthful-looking for forty-five. "You two had a hard life. You, especially."

"I guess." She held Brad's gaze a moment. He knew about her past, of course, because he was married to her sister; after Tessa had been released from prison, she had lived with Janey.

Just the thought of her time in jail made her shiver. Dawson Federal Prison Camp was a minimum security facility, without bars, but the prisoners were locked down at night, performed long tedious work details and had no say over their time. Worse, Tessa had always had a sense of foreboding, as if something bad was going to happen to her. A few times, awful things had…even now, she sometimes woke up in a cold sweat from a bad dream.

Hugging her tighter, Brad whispered, "Don't think about it, kid."

"I try not to."

"Hey, buddy, what are you doing with my wife?"

Tessa and Brad both smiled as Dan approached. He'd just gotten out of the pool, and his muscles were outlined by his T-shirt. Damp from the water, his navy shirt heightened the color of his eyes.

"Just catching up." Brad took a carrot stick from the plate on the table. "I haven't seen her much."

Dan shrugged. "You've been out of town a lot."

"Yeah, this grant thing's great, but it's hell on my life. We had to hire a new internist to take on some of my patients. Janey's been terrific but I know it's hard on her."

"That's what you get for being such a world-renowned researcher."

"Says the hotshot D.A." Brad glanced over at his

wife, who was sprawled in a lounge chair getting some sun. "I wanted to ask you two to watch out for her and the kids. I've got that trip to London coming up, and I'll be gone awhile."

"Of course." Dan's expression grew serious. "Any time."

"I'm sorry I can't get back for the Citizen of the Year dinner. Janey will stay for it, though, and come to London afterward when Oxford officially awards me the grant."

Dan clapped Brad on the back. "It won't be the same without you."

After exchanging more small talk, Brad went to check the meat on the grill, and Tessa and Dan stood watching the kids playing in the pool. Dan's mother, Claire, who'd been taking pictures of them, got up from the poolside bench. At sixty, she was an attractive woman with gray-bobbed hair, youthful skin and a generous smile, though today it seemed forced. "Can I help?" she asked Tessa.

"No, we're waiting on the grill. Want some lemonade?"

"Yes, dear."

While she poured her mother-in-law a glassful, Dan put his arm around Claire's shoulder and kissed her. "You okay?"

She looked up at him. "He's not coming, I guess."

"Nick had a lot going on at the center, Mom. Don't take it personally."

"It *is* personal. He'll never forgive me for how I treated him after your father...left. It happened so long ago, and he's done so much with his life. I wish he could forgive and forget."

Tessa handed her the drink. "He'll come around."

"We Logans can't seem to put the past behind us."

Dan's brow furrowed. "Did something happen?"

His mother sipped the lemonade, then ran her finger around the rim of the glass. "I received a letter from your father's attorney. Daniel's earning money again and wanted to know if we needed anything."

Dan's stance shifted. "Several years too late," he said, his tone clipped. "We worked like dogs to survive after he used up all our money and stole more."

Sometimes when Dan talked about his father, it chilled Tessa. He seemed to turn into a different man, one she didn't really know.

"Be that as it may, I don't want anything from him, but I'd like to stop taking your money, Dan."

"Why?" Tessa asked. "We're not hurting."

"You two could vacation more. Have a new car every few years."

Dan smiled at Tessa. "We've got all we need, don't we, sweetheart?"

"You bet. And we use the money I earn at the library for anything extra we want."

Dan refused to let her put her paycheck toward necessities. Instead she bought frills for the girls, Dan and sometimes herself, and used what was left for vacations, like a weekend away with her husband now and then. One of those was coming up. They were taking a few extra days when Dan had to go to Rockford to give a presentation to the city council on some innovative crime prevention work he'd done with underprivileged kids.

"Steaks are ready," Brad called.

"Come on, Mom, I'll help you find a rare one." Dan grasped her arm and glanced over at Tessa. He mouthed "thank you."

She nodded. She didn't care about the money they gave Claire. No one wanted for anything in her household, and his mother couldn't make ends meet on the hospital aide job she'd taken once she'd retired from full-time work. Though her condo was paid for, she needed other income.

Molly yelled from the pool, "Mom, look!"

Glancing over, Tessa saw her little daredevil do a backflip off the diving board.

Tessa's chest tightened. "Be careful, honey." Too protective, she knew. She had to lighten up.

Janey stood and yelled something to Molly about being careful. She wore a white swimsuit, high-cut at the legs. Tessa was in a navy Speedo swimsuit, with a wraparound skirt tied at her waist…

Buy this bathing suit, Trix. It's sexy as hell.

I don't want to. It's too revealing.

I want you revealed, doll.

No, Frankie.

He'd grabbed her arms.

You're hurting me. What's wrong with you?

Don't say that. Nothing's wrong with me. Why do people keep sayin' that to me?

Although the day was warm, Tessa shivered.

"Honey," Dan called from the grill. "Come on, steaks are ready."

"Be right there. I need to get more drinks." She fled into the kitchen. Her life was wonderful, and she was going to enjoy it. She put on a big fat smile as she took the lemonade concentrate out of Janey's freezer and brought them to the sink.

ALLISON MARKHAM was a striking woman. Her auburn hair, caught up in a twist, accented the flawless perfection of her face. She was dressed in her customary tailored suit. At one time, Dan had loved the cool sophistication Allison seemed to have been born with. He chuckled to himself at how he ever thought this woman could make him happy.

"I won't plea down on this case, Dan. Your offer is insulting."

He shook his head. "It's the only one you're going to get. Your client is a criminal, Allison, no matter how white his collar is. He cheated senior citizens out of their pensions."

Her expression softened, and she hitched a hip on

his desk. He got a hint of the French perfume she always wore. "That's why you're being such a hard-ass about this. Because it kicks in to what your father did."

"No, because Sam Albert belongs behind bars. You should be working to keep scum like him out of business, not set him free so he can trick more people on a fixed income."

Anger sparked in her gray eyes. He should have known better. Allison gave as good as she got, both in her professional and personal life. "Doesn't it get tiring, keeping that halo in place?"

Looking down at his desk, Dan counted to ten. You'd think after all this time, Allison would let up on him. But, no, she was still steamed that he'd broken it off with her for Tessa. And her attitude had seemed to worsen in recent months. Probably because Allison's marriage had ended not too long ago. Rumors had spread that it was an acrimonious split. He guessed that would make anybody sour. And maybe it made sense to take out her issues on Dan—in truth, they could have been married and she'd never have gone through the divorce.

Regardless, he wasn't going to back down on this case. He looked her square in the eye. "This meeting is over. I refuse to discuss my personal life with you or anyone else. The offer on Albert stands. Take it or leave it."

"I'll let you know."

"It's only on the table for today."

Damn it, he hadn't planned to say that. But Allison could push his buttons.

"You've got to be kidding."

"Sorry, I'm not."

She pushed off from the desk and glowered at him. "Someday, something's going to bring you down, Dan. You're going to find out you're no better than everyone else."

"I don't think I'm better than anyone else. Far from it."

"Get real. I hope you and your perfect wife are ready for the fall when it happens."

Man, that divorce really *had* soured her. For a minute, he was frozen with fear. He'd never be able to handle it if something caused him and Tessa to split. Hell, why was he worrying? Things had never been better between them. Nothing was going to change that.

THE FREAKIN' TOWN could have come off a postcard. From the bus, Frankie watched the quiet streets pass by—quaint houses alongside the downtown businesses. It reminded him of a picture book he'd had when he was little. He was sick a lot as a kid and had to stay in bed. Once, a priest from the church near his house had brought him a book. It was about God and how He helped a little town. Frankie loved that story. When he was alone at night and scared, he still talked to God.

He got off at the Orchard Place Station, wondering what the hell must have happened to make Trixie leave Iverton. He felt for the letter in his pocket. The last time she wrote to him, she asked him to come to Orchard Place and rescue her. He smiled as he navigated the steps. That was what Frankie was going to do here—save Trixie.

Though it was four in the afternoon, he put on his sunglasses and the fishing hat that he had bought at one of the places the bus had stopped on the trip east. No need to make his presence known yet; just his luck he'd bump into Janey. He looked the same as he had when he'd last seen her, screaming at him after the trial.

I hate you, you bastard.

Shut up, bitch.

Maybe on this visit he could get back at her for saying those things to him, and for poisoning Trixie's mind against him. *She* must have brought Trixie here. His beloved wouldn't have come of her own free will. It made him sick inside not knowing where she was and what she was doing. He had to find out what Trixie had gotten herself into in this Hicksville.

He went inside the station proper and up to the counter. He hated places like this. They suffocated him. That's why, all his life, Frankie had had to own a car, so he could avoid depressing places like this. He'd had beauties when he was on the outside, which always made him feel like somebody. First thing he was going to do when he found Trixie was get some new wheels.

"Can I help you?" the man behind the plastic asked. He was a weasel of a guy with a bad comb-over.

"Yeah, I need a room to stay for a few days. Where's the nearest hotel?" He didn't have a lot of money, but he expected Trixie could get what they'd need to keep them going for a while.

"There's a couple of bed and breakfasts on the outskirts of town." The guy shrugged. "Nice if you like company. They serve communal meals."

That was the last thing Frankie wanted. "Nah, somethin' with more privacy."

"There's a hotel in the center of town. It's not the newest, but it's clean and private. Name's Heritage House."

"Thanks." Frankie started to walk away.

"What's your business here?" the guy called after him.

"None of yours."

He wouldn't give himself away—he wanted to surprise Trixie. He could picture her running to him like in those old TV commercials and throwing herself into his arms. And later, the sex would be hot and rough like she liked it.

As he left the bus station, a man in tattered clothes came up to him. "Any spare change, buddy?"

Frankie looked down at the guy. Homeless probably. Because Frankie remembered what it was like to be hungry and have nowhere he belonged, he dug in his pocket. Handing the guy a bill, he said, "Don't spend it on booze."

"Sure thing. Thanks, mister."

The thought of some booze right now sounded good to Frankie. He glanced up and down the street. Then he saw a bar two doors over with a dark interior and a neon sign announcing Zip's Café. In the window was a beer sign.

Dodging oncoming cars, Frankie crossed the street. Before he went looking for Trixie, he could use a belt or two to calm his nerves. Just the thought of seeing her made him jittery. And sometimes, his mind got cloudy and he didn't remember things right. Especially when his cold was acting up. But alcohol always let him see things clearer.

Inside it was cool and a chill ran through Frankie. He sneezed several times. Setting his duffel bag on a stool, he drew out the black sweater Trixie had sent him for his birthday one year and shrugged into it.

He took a seat at the bar.

"What can I get you?" the bartender asked.

"Whiskey. A double."

The man filled a glass and slid it to him. He knocked the liquor back in one swallow and ordered a second. Warmer and happier, he studied the bar. Not many patrons, as it was almost the dinner hour. Most of the working stiffs in this town were probably hurrying home for boring dinners with their overweight wives and whiny kids. At one time, Frankie had thought he wanted all that. But years of shuffling from foster home to foster home had cured him of the dream. Family members did despicable things to each other.

The man on the stool next to him stood, threw some money on the bar and called goodbye to the bartender. He'd left behind a newspaper. *The Orchard Place Globe* was a hefty size for a small town. He skimmed the front page's national news, read about the most recent hurricane in Florida and another attack in Iraq. What a crummy world. Nowhere was safe anymore. Chaplain Cook told them once that a lot of guys got out of prison and went right back in because they couldn't deal with the real world. Not him, though. When he had Trixie again, he'd be fine.

He flipped through to the local news. Maybe there'd be something in there about Janey's husband, the famous doctor.

Frankie read the front page. The feature article was on a guy…holy hell. The world spun out of focus for a minute, and drums began to beat in his head. He clutched the paper so hard his fists hurt. He heard himself moan, as if from a distance.

"You all right, buddy?" the bartender asked. "You look like you've seen a ghost."

It was Trixie. His Trixie. Only she wasn't alone. She was with two little girls. Behind them, a man stood—tall, imposing, confident. His hand rested possessively on Trixie's shoulder. Frankie had to gulp in air. His gaze dropped to the caption.

"Orchard Place's D.A. honored as 2006 Citizen of the Year. Shown here with wife, Tessa, and two daughters, Molly and Sara. Dinner to be held…"

The print blurred and pain shot to his temples. Tessa? There was that name again. This was his Trixie. She was married? There had to be some mistake. He pulled the picture he'd downloaded from Brad Christopher's Web site out of his wallet.

The two photos matched.

"I don't understand," he murmured.

"What?" the bartender asked.

He shoved his picture out of sight and held up the newspaper. "Who are these people?"

"The Logan family. Pillars of the community. The guy's the town's D.A. and even my ex likes the wife, and she hates most people."

"Her name's Trixie, right?"

"No, Tessa, like it says there. Tessa Logan."

Tessa Logan. This was the love of his life, whose letters had kept him going all these years. How could she be married to somebody else? What the hell was going on here?

He stumbled out of the bar. There had to be a mistake.

"ALL RIGHT, who'd like to start?" Tessa smiled at the four who were part of the Sassy Girls Book Club.

She'd let them pick the name of their group but had taken it upon herself to choose the books. The one for today was from the adolescent literature genre she'd been steering them to since Nick had asked her to be library liaison and, she suspected, a positive role model for these girls. That made her shake her head, but she did want to help, so she forged ahead, squelching her insecurity.

She made eye contact with each teen: Beth, Chelsea, Dawn and Jill. When no one answered her question, she asked, "Did you read the book?"

One by one, they nodded.

At last, Beth spoke up. "I thought it was sad. That girl had everything going for her and still she committed suicide."

Tessa knew a bit about their lives from offhanded statements they'd made. Beth came from a large family on welfare.

Out of the corner of her eye, Tessa saw someone enter the library. She and the girls were sitting in a glassed-in meeting room in the front of the building. Tessa hoped Annie, the night librarian, would take care of the late-afternoon patrons.

She brought her attention back to the teens. "Does everybody think Mina had everything?"

"I don't." This from Dawn, whose parents had gone through a difficult divorce, which led to her rebellious behavior at school. "She had material things—clothes, a car, a big house—but she was lonely."

"I wouldn't change places with her." Jill's husky voice belied her delicate appearance. She was adopted and wanted to search for her birth parents, but her adoptive parents objected. She acted out at school.

Tessa glanced to her left. She'd been waiting for Chelsea's opinion of the main character because Tessa had chosen the book partly because of her. She sensed the girl was not only pregnant but desperate. "Chels, what do you think?"

"I think her boyfriend was a bastard. And her father wasn't much better." With a disgusted look on her face, she added, "All men are pigs, as far as I'm concerned."

From there the girls talked about fathers—what made a good one, a bad one, was a bad one better than none at all? They all spoke in general terms.

Then Chelsea turned to her. The teen's blue eyes were intense. "What about your father, Mrs. L? What was he like? Cool? He had to be because you're so together."

For a moment, Tessa panicked. She never talked about her family, or lack of it. "I, um…" Four faces focused on her. It was then she realized this was some kind of test of trust.

Damned if she was going to fail. "I never knew my father. He took off when I was born."

The girls were shocked.

Chelsea frowned. "I wouldn't have guessed."

Because I've spent my whole life covering things like that up. The burden of keeping that secret was heavy, and Tessa felt like a phony.

"I guess you can come from a dysfunctional family and still be a happy adult," she told them.

"Was yours?" Dawn asked. "Dysfunctional?"

"Yes." She kept her voice calm. "Maybe you'd like to share some of your background with me?"

The girls relayed much of what Tessa already knew about them. Poverty, depression, frustration and loneliness combined to send them into a downward spiral.

Chelsea, however, refused to share. "Can we talk about the book?"

By the time the girls left, Tessa felt like she had accomplished something important. The bond they'd been forming all year had strengthened, and they seemed to take comfort in it. Hard as it was, she was right to share her story.

Could she have some impact on the boys? She hadn't followed up on Nick's request a few weeks ago. How long was she going to let Frankie affect her life? She'd call Nick tomorrow to talk about a group for the guys.

After locking up the meeting room, Tessa headed down the long corridor to the office. The library had been built in the early 1900s, and, though she loved its quaint atmosphere, the corridors tended to get dark as the day wore on. She thought she saw something in the shadows. "Who's there?" she asked, her heart pounding.

No answer.

Of course there was no answer. She was letting talk of her past spook her. Swallowing hard, she found her office and opened the door. She stopped when she heard another noise. Then she saw a man, his back to her, striding down the hall and out the front door. There was something familiar about his walk.

CHAPTER FIVE

DAN WAS DETERMINED to keep his temper as he drove to Molly's school. Tessa was chaperoning a field trip to the zoo with Sara's class, and the elementary school principal had called him about yet another incident concerning his older daughter. Molly was always stirring things up at school—causing some kind of ruckus on the playground, planning pranks, daring the other kids to stretch the rules. The incidents were invariably harmless, but she was making a name for herself with the faculty.

This time, though, her actions were more serious. She'd cheated on a test. In fourth grade! Dan was shocked when the principal, Katie Gardner, someone he and Nick had gone to school with, called to tell him what had happened. He was more than a little disappointed in Molly. But as he pulled up to the building and headed inside, he curbed his reaction. He knew he tended to overreact to anything resembling public embarrassment, and Molly would need a sane parent now. The secretary showed him to the appropriate office.

Katie, a pretty blonde, sat behind her desk with Molly across from her. His little girl swung her sneakered feet back and forth, staring down at her hands in her lap.

Katie looked over at him. "Hi, Dan."

Molly didn't acknowledge his arrival. He greeted Katie then crossed to his daughter. Kneeling in front of her, he said, "Mol, what happened?"

She kept staring at her lap and so he tilted her chin. Her eyes were red-rimmed and her usually smiling face distraught. She bit her lip, the vulnerable gesture making her father's heart ache. "I...I..."

She threw herself at him and sobbed into his chest. He held on to her solid little body and let her cry. Lord knew this wasn't the worst thing that could happen, but he was glad she was showing repentance. Or maybe it was fear. They'd had stern talks with both girls about fairness, integrity and doing your own work. When the outburst subsided, still holding on to her, he sank into a chair.

Katie gave him a sympathetic smile.

He smoothed down his daughter's hair. "We need to talk about this, kiddo."

She shook her head.

"Yes, we do." After one more hug, he set her in her own chair. "Mrs. Gardner says you cheated on a test."

Molly wouldn't look at him.

"Why, Molly? You're a good student. You know your math. Why would you cheat?"

"Sammy asked me," she said at last, still averting her gaze.

"Sammy?"

When she didn't answer, Katie filled Dan in. "Samantha Carter. A very popular girl. She copied off Molly's paper. With Molly's prior consent."

"That's not really cheating," Molly whined.

"Of course it is, honey." When he received no response, Dan said, "Molly, look at me. It *is* cheating to let someone copy your work. But I think you already know that, don't you?"

An expression of childish mutiny flashed across her face. "Nuh-uh."

"Well, then, we have a problem. If you don't think you did something wrong…"

She started to cry again. "I did. It was wrong. I guess I didn't think it was cheating."

"Now that's progress." Katie studied her. "At least you know you did something wrong. Why did you, Molly?"

"I dunno."

"Molly?" Obviously, the principal knew something.

"I wanna go to Sammy's birthday party next month."

"And you wanted to get her to like you by allowing her to copy off your paper?" Katie asked.

"Yeah, I guess."

Now Dan understood. Peer pressure to cheat.

Katie's expression was firm but kind. "What do you think would be an appropriate punishment, Molly? Here at school?"

"A zero on the test. That's what Ms. Altman said we were both gonna get." He saw his daughter's hand fist. She hated to fail at anything and had signs of becoming the perfectionist that he was. The notion made him uncomfortable.

"That's a given, Molly. What else?"

Her brow furrowed. "Stay after school, for that thing you started."

"After-school community service." Katie said to Dan, "If kids do something wrong, instead of making them sit in detention, we have a program where we arrange for them to help the community in some way."

"That's a terrific idea." The penal system could take pointers from this elementary school.

She smiled. "It was your brother's idea at one of our PTA meetings last year. Nick came as a speaker from the Center for At-Risk Teens to talk to parents about how to keep kids on track."

Dan wondered why Nick hadn't told him—and how he'd missed that meeting. Maybe Tessa had gone. "It sounds like a remarkable program. Just let us know what Molly has to do, and we'll make arrangements for transportation."

"Fine." Katie stood and circled the desk. "Molly, people make mistakes. I hope you learn from this one. And be warned. A second infraction carries a lot more punishment."

"Yes, Mrs. Gardner."

Dan took Molly's hand and led her to the car. Once inside and buckled into their seats, he asked, "You okay?"

She began to cry again.

"Molly, as Mrs. Gardner said, people make mistakes. It's important to learn from them. Not make them again."

"Mommy'll be disappointed."

"Yes, she will. That's what happens when you do the wrong thing."

"Are you?"

"Uh-huh." He tightened his hold on her hand. "But you know what? When people are disappointed, they get over it, especially if the person shows remorse. And it's important not to hold grudges."

She frowned. "Uncle Nick has a grudge against Grandma. And you got a grudge against Grandpa."

Dan froze with the key midway to the engine. "How do you know all that about grudges?"

"I heard Mom and Grandma talking."

He'd never explained to his kids about his family history. "Like I told you before, my father doesn't live here, Mol, so none of us has seen him in years. And if I do have a grudge, I'm working on getting over it." Was he? "Now back to you. If you promise you won't do this again, that will go a long way in making us less disappointed."

"'Kay." Her impish look was back. "So no punishment at home?"

"Sorry, Mol. There will be. We have to consult Mom." He glanced at his watch. "Let's stop at the park near the house. You and I can spend some time together." Something he didn't do enough of these days. "Then we'll go and talk to Mom."

As much as Dan hated that his daughter cheated, he felt sorry for the poor kid. She was usually so cheerful. And people did make mistakes. God knew he'd been living with one for years. He banished the thought of Molly's admonition about grudges.

At the park, he removed his tie and jacket to play catch with Molly—he kept a ball and mitts in the car. Then he pushed her on the swings. When he was tired out, he said, "Why don't you go to the jungle gym for a while. I'm going to sit on the bench."

She flung her arms around him. "Okay, Daddy."

Dan watched her for a while, soothed by the rich earthy scent of the grass, the sound of birds in nearby trees and the sight of his daughter climbing the iron bars like a monkey. When she jumped into the sandbox, Dan took out his BlackBerry handheld and checked his e-mail. He was halfway through his list when he glanced up and saw Molly talking to a man. Dan was off the bench and beside her in seconds.

"No, my dad's here, too."

Dan put his hand on Molly's shoulder. "Is there a problem here?"

The guy was about fifty, gray hair, an almost wizened face. He wore a black sweater and ratty jeans. "No problem. Just asked the little girl if there were any ducks on the pond."

"I told him you said never to talk to strangers, Dad."

He gave the man his most piercing look. "Did you just move into this neighborhood? I've never seen you at our park before."

"Nah, just got into town."

"What are you doing here?"

The guy shrugged and started away.

"You should know better than to approach young girls in the park," Dan called after him. "I'm the D.A. in town, and we don't like it when strangers accost children."

The man glanced over his shoulder. "Cool it, buddy. No *accosting* goin' on here."

"Who was that?"

Dan turned to see his neighbor down the street, with her three little kids, all smaller than Molly. "I have no idea, Pam. But watch your children. I have a bad feeling about him."

That was an understatement. The guy made his skin crawl.

AT 6:00 A.M., Tessa dragged herself out of bed, leaving Dan sprawled, sound asleep. His face was relaxed like it seldom was when he was awake, and a stubble of beard shadowed his jaw. Last night, she'd kissed that jaw with abandon...

"What's that for?" he'd asked as they were getting ready for bed. They were both in the bathroom. He'd showered and dried off, when she'd sidled in front of him. Kissed his jaw.

"Because I love you." She hadn't stopped there. She'd moved her mouth to his chest, licking off stray drops of water.

"Oh, man. That feels terrific." She'd wedged her hand between them and cupped him, startling him. "Tessa, what?"

"You're wonderful, Dan. A great lover..." She'd begun to massage him. "A terrific husband, and not the least of all, a number one dad."

"Ah, now I get it." He'd leaned against the wall as she'd explored him.

"You handled Molly so well. I know how much you abhor any kind of cheating and lying, but you were great with her. Just the right combination of firmness and gentleness."

"Tessa?" he'd said, his voice a growl.

"Hmm?"

"Let's not talk about Molly anymore."

She'd given him her best sexy laugh, which had earned her a passionate kiss and a hurried trip to their bed....

Dan rolled over on his side; Tessa tiptoed to the

bathroom and dressed in light sweats. By six-thirty, she met Janey at the park, at a halfway point between their houses. It was a gray and overcast morning, but the cool air would make their walk more comfortable. Every Monday, Wednesday and Friday they met in the same spot. Tessa valued these mornings alone with Janey, getting exercise and still arriving home in time to get the kids ready for school.

"Hey, Janey. Love that hot pink sweat suit." Her sister looked adorable. "When'd you get it?"

"Last week. Fields was having a sale. I would have bought you one if I thought you'd wear this color."

Tessa glanced down at her gray outfit. "This is fine for me."

They began at a slow pace. "Did Brad leave?"

"Yeah. He took the eleven o'clock flight last night. Boy, I hate his being gone so much. I always feel unanchored."

"He's part of you, that's why."

"I know. I have a hell of a time making decisions without him. Sometimes I'm afraid I've gotten to depend on him too much." She sighed. "I guess I'll have to get used to being on my own for a while."

Holding her three pound hand weights, Tessa clumsily touched Janey's hand. "I'll be here for you, Janey."

"I know."

"Want to come over with the boys for dinner

tonight? Dan's making barbecued chicken, Nick's favorite. He's coming, too."

"Jimmy has baseball practice until six, but after that?"

"Sure."

They picked up their pace as Janey asked, "So how's the little criminal holding up?"

Tessa stopped and stared at her sister.

Janey clapped a hand over her mouth. "Oh, my God, honey, I'm sorry. I don't know why I'd say something like that to you."

"No, it's okay. I'm too sensitive. Dan and I both are."

Falling back in stride, Janey asked, "How'd he handle her cheating?"

"He was kind to her and stayed with her last night until she fell asleep. He even figured out how to ground her so she'll miss enough to feel the pain but won't miss the girl scout camping trip."

"He's a gem."

Tessa smiled over at her sister. "He— Oh, what…"

A jogger coming from behind bumped Tessa's shoulder, making her stumble off the path and drop her hand weights.

"Watch where you're going!" Janey yelled after the guy.

The jogger grunted. He wore a navy hooded sweatshirt so they couldn't see his face. Janey scowled. "That was rude."

"Probably needs his morning caffeine."

"Probably."

"Now, enough about me. How's it going with the fund-raiser for Brad's project?"

"Super. I could use some help, though."

As Tessa listened to her sister outline the gala, she glanced down the path. The man had disappeared, outran them, she guessed.

OH, GOD...OH, GOD...OH, GOD. He couldn't believe it. He'd touched her. She'd felt more solid than before and looked heavier, but she was still as beautiful as ever. She might have to lose a few pounds, but he couldn't wait to run his hands over every inch of her.

He waited behind a copse of trees. He was cold, and his nose was runny, but he stayed where he was. Maybe he could get another glimpse of her. He'd been trailing her for days. He'd checked out the library, where he'd gotten his first real look at her, but there were people milling around and it was too public. She walked with her stupid sister every other morning. But Frankie was hoping Janey might not be here today. No such luck. If Trixie had been alone, he was prepared to snatch her. His hands itched.

He'd been in town a week, and followed her everywhere—except for the day he'd been really sick and had had to stay in bed. He'd even written down her routine. Cripes, he couldn't believe it. Trixie had a totally boring life, which would drive him crazy. She worked at that crummy library, and she drove those damn kids everywhere. She even had something to do with the local teen center. No wonder she'd written to him to take her away from all this drudgery.

When he'd been driving his rented car by the school her kids went to, he'd seen that bastard who'd stolen her away come out of the building with one of them. He'd followed them to the park, and couldn't resist talking to the little girl when dumbo was checking his mini computer.

The kid looked just like Trixie. Same color eyes, hair, which even curled like Trixie's used to—though she wasn't wearing it like that these days. Frankie had been so stunned by their resemblance, he didn't see that guy approach them. Frankie had made up some stupid question and had got out of there fast.

He stuck his head out from behind the big oak and saw they were coming up. His heart began to hammer and he grabbed on to a low tree limb to steady himself. And pretty soon…there they were.

"You're kidding right?" Trixie said and laughed out loud.

Oh, God, her voice was like an angel's.

"No, I…" Janey stopped fast. "Did you see that?"

"What?"

"I don't know, something behind those trees?"

"I didn't see anything."

"I thought I did." She shook herself. "I guess the gray day has me spooked."

They started walking again, but Frankie didn't dare risk looking again until he was sure they'd gone.

That's okay. He wasn't planning to wait much longer to take her away from all this.

DAN'S ASSISTANT, WANDA, entered his office holding the flyer she'd typed up and duplicated. "Here they are, Dan." She hesitated.

"What?"

"I was wondering if you were maybe making too much of this guy in the park?"

"Probably." He did feel somewhat foolish. "But with my kids, I'd rather appear rash than regret not doing something later on. And we do have a Neighborhood Watch."

"I suppose it wouldn't hurt to pass these out."

"Maybe I'll check with someone first. I don't want to alarm the parents on my block."

Wanda gave him a very female grin. "Try that cute brother of yours. He has his pulse on things like this."

"Great idea."

Dan punched in Nick's cell as soon as Wanda left.

"Logan."

"Nick, it's Dan. Do you have a minute? I need your opinion on something."

"Yeah, shoot."

"There was this guy in the park near our house yesterday afternoon. He approached Molly. Talked to her. Asked her a dumb question about the ducks."

"Where were *you?*"

"About twenty yards away, reading my e-mail on my BlackBerry. I should have been more watchful."

"No, I didn't ask because of that. If a guy came up to her in full view of you, it might have a different spin."

"How so?"

"He wouldn't do anything if you were right there. Unless he's some kind of psycho."

"Is that your MSW talking?"

"Yeah, it is. Now, can I speak as an uncle?"

"I wish you would. You know how overprotective I am. But this thing has been bothering me all morning."

"As Molly's uncle, I think you should take it seriously."

"To the extent of passing out flyers about him?" He glanced at the notices, adding wryly, "Which I've already had duplicated, by the way."

Nick chuckled. "Hell, pass them out. Everybody on your street already thinks you're the world's greatest dad. The mothers will love you even more."

"Bite me."

"Back at you, big brother."

Dan eased a hip on his desk. "We missed you Sunday."

"Yeah? I was busy."

"With what?"

"I had a date Saturday night, if you must know. I didn't want to bound out of bed for a family picnic."

"That would be good news if it was the truth."

"It is."

"Who was the girl?"

He hesitated. "I don't kiss and tell."

"You were avoiding Mom."

"That, too."

Dan wondered if he should tell Nick what his mother had said. What the hell? "Dad's lawyer contacted her."

Stone-cold silence.

"He wanted to know if Mom needed money."

"Does she? I have some saved if she needs it."

"No, she's fine in that department. What do you think the bastard's up to?" Given the ill feeling simply talking about his father conjured, he guessed Molly was right about his grudge.

"I have no idea. And I don't care." Silence again. "Look, I'll check around here at the center about the guy you saw in the park. Maybe he's turned up elsewhere. Give me the description."

Dan rattled off what he'd put on the flyer. As he fleshed out the stranger's looks for Nick, Dan got angry. If anyone tried to hurt his kid—or his wife—Dan knew he could do anything to anybody to protect them.

CHAPTER SIX

"BREATHE IN. Slowly let the air out. The tension will drain from your body with each exhalation." The voice of François, the owner and premier teacher at The Yoga Experience, was as soothing as his message. "Don't dwell on anything but your breathing. Don't think about life or your responsibilities or your problems."

Eyes closed, Tessa sat cross-legged, spine straight, head up, hands open at her hips. By concentrating on breathing, she could usually block everything else. But not today. Not after her fight with Dan....

"Why on earth didn't you tell me yesterday, before you distributed *these* to the neighborhood?" She'd held up a flyer.

"I didn't want to upset you."

"I'm not a fragile china doll, Dan. Treat me like an adult."

For the rest of the evening, they'd been cool to each other. But he should have told her....

"All right, now we'll go into some asanas. First, downward dog."

Tessa got on all fours, straightened her arms and went into a crouch. Stretching her back, legs and spine, she assumed one of the most basic poses in yoga.

"I hate to fight like this," Dan had said in bed after they turned off the lights.

"I know. Me, too."

"I'm sorry."

She sighed. "If there was less resentment in your voice, I might believe you."

"Damn it, Tessa, I'm trying to protect my family…."

This morning, things had been better. Dan had made them breakfast, and the atmosphere in the house was congenial. She'd kissed Dan and the girls goodbye at eight-thirty.

Every Saturday when he didn't have to work overtime, Dan spent a few hours alone with Molly and Sara. It gave them time together without her, and Tessa got to take a yoga class and afterward go shopping or once in a while get a manicure or massage. She tried to return the favor, giving Dan the opportunity to play golf on Saturday or Sunday or go out with his brother.

"Tessa, are you well?" François asked in his distinct French accent at the end of class.

"Yes, of course, why?"

"You were distracted today."

She picked up her mat and rolled it. "I didn't realize it showed."

"You fidgeted during the resting poses. This is not like you."

"I'll be better next time. Thanks for caring."

She returned the belt, bolster and mat to their assigned places and trundled down the steep staircase from the loft. Humming softly, she headed to her SUV, which they'd gotten back from the shop yesterday. The damage had been severe but could have been so much worse. Shivering, she reached for the door. She had it open before she realized she hadn't used the remote unlocking device. Odd. She *had* locked up the car. She always locked it.

"Hell," she said, starting the engine. If she was distracted enough for François to notice, she couldn't be sure she had locked the car.

Laughing at her skittishness, she decided to go over to Park Avenue to her favorite little diner and have coffee. Then she'd hit the sweet shop across the street and get the girls and Dan some candy. Placing the car in Reverse and releasing the brake, she checked the rearview mirror to back out.

"Hello, Trixie."

Tessa slammed on the brakes. Her heart catapulted in her chest as she saw the man's face in the mirror. She gripped the steering wheel, scenarios of stalkers and criminals and what they did to their victims running through her head.

Then she realized the significance of what the man said.

Trixie. He said *Trixie.* There was only one person in the world who'd ever called her that. It was his pet name for her. Too stunned to speak, she stared into the rearview mirror at Frankie Hamilton. At least she thought it must be him. He bore little resemblance to the boy she had known in Iverton, Ohio. The mixed-up boy who, because he showed her attention and gave her compliments, she'd almost thrown away her future for.

"What's the matter, doll?"

She swallowed hard, tried to take in air, her gaze transfixed on the mirror.

"There's a deserted parking lot around the corner," he said. "Drive there."

When she remained immobile, he barked, "Now!"

That tone of voice, that ability to change from nice guy to crazy man in the blink of an eye, had scared her to death when she was nineteen.

It still did.

Her hands clammy, she ordered herself to be calm. Easing her foot off the brake, she backed up, turned the car around and drove out of the parking area. Too soon, she found the lot he'd indicated. There wasn't a single car in it, and all the windows in the building were dark.

"Shut off the engine."

Like a robot, she did as she was told. Fear knotted her stomach as the ramifications of Frankie Hamilton's showing up in Orchard Place began to sink in.

FROWNING, FRANKIE GOT OUT of the van and circled to the driver side, cursing the slight drizzle that had just begun. He opened the door for her, but Trixie stayed where she was. What was the matter with her? Why wasn't she squealing with delight, flinging herself into his arms? She'd begged him to come and rescue her. "Trixie, baby, get outta the car."

When she continued to stare at him from the seat, he saw fear in those pretty, hazel eyes. He didn't understand it. Must be she was shocked to see him. But why would she be? She asked him to get her out of here. Confused, his head began to hurt. "Come on, unsnap the seatbelt."

Finally she moved.

He reached out to help her down, and she drew back. "Don't."

What the hell?

Once she got on the ground, he moved toward her. She stepped backward until she hit the van. Her hands were braced by her sides and her eyes were wide.

He came in so close he could see the sweat beading above her lip. "God, you smell great." He sniffed her hair. "It's somethin' different than what you used to use." Smiling, he lowered his head for the kiss he'd been dreaming about for fifteen years.

"No!" She pushed his chest, unbalancing him. Then she darted around him and started to run. She wore sneakers and some stupid-looking pants and shirt so she wasn't bogged down by jeans and boots like he was. But Frankie caught up to her behind the building. Yanking her back by the hair, he stopped her cold. She screamed again but shut up when he threw her up against the concrete, banging her head. The blow knocked the wind out of her, but after she caught her breath she fought him, trying to get away.

"Stop it! What's the matter with you?"

Again, he rammed her up against the building and backhanded her as hard as he could—twice, on her left cheek. Tears sprang to her eyes. "Don't make me hurt you worse, Trixie. You know I will."

Finally, she stopped struggling. He expected her to cry and apologize, as she always had, but instead her eyes narrowed on him and she pulled herself up straight. "What do you want?"

He cocked his head. "I came to get you, doll."

"*Get* me?"

"Yeah. You know, like you asked me to in your letters."

Her brow furrowed as if she didn't understand. He hated when people looked at him like that, as if he was saying something crazy. Chaplain Cook told him to ignore those looks, but he couldn't all the time.

"What letters?" she asked.

"Come on, Trix. The ones you wrote me in prison."

"Frankie, I never wrote you one letter in prison. We had no contact after the trial."

"Now why would you lie about something like that?" His head began to hurt at the base of the skull. "You know I don't like it when you lie." He gripped her tightly and studied her face where a bruise was forming on her cheek. "Is that why you're sayin' this? Because I hit you?"

"No, it's the truth."

"It isn't."

He grabbed her by the wrists and started to drag her away. "We'll go back to my hotel, and I'll show them letters to you."

"I'm not going anywhere with you. You're crazy."

Spots swam before his eyes. In the haze, he saw his father bat him on the side of the head. Blow after blow. Some woman in the background yelled, *Don't do that, Stan! You'll make something go wrong in the head with him.*

He's already crazy, his father said, just before his fist connected again.

"You come with me, Trixie, or I'm goin' over to 19 Kilmer Drive to knock on that slate-blue door of yours. Then the bastard that you're with will answer it. Or maybe that cute little girl with curls like yours will answer first. Maybe Daddy's asleep. Maybe…"

"Shut up!" Tessa said.

He had to hit her again.

"All right, I'll come with you."

Smiling serenely, he said, "Now, that's my girl."

"HERE, PUT THIS on your cheek."

Tessa stared at the man. He'd made her an ice pack for a bruise *he'd* inflicted. He *was* crazy. When they were young, he went in and out of these moods. Savage fury to unexpected tenderness. He was often sick with allergies and asthma, too, but he was nice when she took care of him. Then, without warning, Mr. Hyde appeared and scared her to death. And there was no one to go to for help. Janey was only six years older, and Tessa had been afraid Frankie might hurt her sister. Janey had been vocal enough about hating Frankie. If she'd known what he'd done to her on a regular basis, Janey would have gone after him bodily. But after an episode he'd get all nice, and Tessa would think everything was going to be all right. It boggled her mind how mixed up she had been then.

She wasn't that naive now, though she was shaken beyond belief by his return.

Keep calm, she told herself. *He's dangerous. Just see what he wants*. So she took the ice and said, "Thanks."

"Sit down."

The sight of the bed made her stomach cramp. What was he planning? She pulled out the straight chair from the desk and sat.

He rummaged around in a duffel bag on the dresser, tossing things out of it. A black sweater. A blue hooded sweatshirt. The sight of them made her gasp. The jogger in the park last week had worn a blue hoody. The man Dan saw with Molly had worn a black sweater. Had she unknowingly endangered her daughter?

"You've been following me. My family."

"Family?"

"My husband and daughter."

"You don't have a family, Trixie. You've been waitin' for me. All these years."

He drew something out of the bag and placed it on the bed. A stack of letters. He held on to another stack. When he turned around, his face was beaming. "See, these are all the letters you sent me."

"Frankie, I didn't—"

His face reddened, and his eyes bulged. "Don't make me hurt you again."

Oh, God, she was going to have enough trouble explaining her bruised face. It throbbed, so it had to look horrendous.

"I won't." She nodded to the letters. "Let me see them."

As she took the stack from him, she noticed his hands were muscled and beefy. His whole body was. Much more than when they were young. What damage could he inflict on her now? She scanned her surroundings. Had she been foolish to come to this musty-smelling hotel with him? To this room in a deserted corridor? If she hadn't come with him, he would have gone to Dan. Or maybe he'd hurt Molly. Tessa had to placate him, even if she put herself at risk, until she could get him to leave town. Surely he would when she made it clear she wasn't going with him.

Take calming breaths. Like in yoga.

With one hand holding the ice to her cheek, she put the stack of letters on her lap and leafed through them. They were all addressed to Franklin R. Hamilton, Kansas Federal Penitentiary. But they weren't in her handwriting. Of course they weren't. And there was no postmark. A frightening suspicion took root in her brain. Setting the ice pack on the floor, she opened one of the letters.

Dear Frankie,
How are you today? I dreamed about you last night…

She halted, unable to read the filth that followed, so she skimmed over it. At the end, the letter read:

I love you and am waiting for you. I count the days until we can be together.
Yours always,
Trixie.

What this meant hit her with sledgehammer force. How should she deal with this…aberration? This lunacy?

"See, doll, I told you. You just don't remember writing those, do you?"

"Uh, no, Frankie, I don't remember."

His eyes seemed unfocused. "You been sick, baby? Is that why?"

"I'm not sure." She went on instinct. "Frankie, I married somebody else. Maybe I was sick when I did that, but I have another life now. A family."

The haze cleared and he went from crazy-looking to sane. "I know. You did a bad thing."

"Regardless, I did it."

"You have to undo it."

"I can't."

"You have to." His hands fisted at his sides, and she worried he might hit her again. "You don't love him."

She didn't respond.

"Trixie. Did you hear me?"

"I can't leave my daughters, Frankie. I do love them. God wouldn't want a mother to leave her children."

"God?" He thought for a minute, remembering Chaplain Cook's talk about God and family, picturing the Catholic priest who had been nice to him when he was young. "Maybe not." His expression changed to one of delight. "We'll have a kid of our own when we go away. But I want a boy."

She shivered. "I'm sorry, Frankie, I can't go anywhere with you."

"Does the guy know? About your past?"

"Yes, of course."

"I don't believe that. You freaked when I said I was goin' over there."

"He doesn't like to think about it. He's a powerful man in this town. You should stay away from him."

"What do I get if I do?"

Oh, Lord, help me please. "Money."

"Huh?"

"You can't have much, after all those years in prison. I'll give you money to start a new life."

"Maybe I need some money. To buy us a car." He frowned. "I miss my cars. I feel better when I have my own."

"I remember. I can get you enough for a used one. You can go somewhere and start a new life."

"Okay."

She breathed a sigh of relief.

"We can go away together if I have a car and some extra cash."

"I said I can't go with you, Frankie."

He grabbed her by the wrist. "You have to come with me."

"No, Frankie. Please, God, no."

He sat down on the bed and put his hands to his temples. "I dunno. I dunno. God might…" He rubbed up and down. "Maybe. Maybe. Let's start with the money. The car." He looked up at her. "I gotta think about the rest of this. But my head hurts now." He sneezed. "And I don't feel good."

"Why don't you lie down?"

"Okay. Tuck me in, take care of me like you used to?"

She cringed. "Sure."

He slid onto the bed and stretched out. His face, his position, were that of a child's taking a nap; she pulled the spread over him. "Tomorrow," he said. "Come here. In the morning."

"I can't. It's Sunday, I can't get away."

"N-no. T-tomorrow."

"Frankie, I have to go to church. And there are meetings afterward I have to attend."

"Okay. Church is important. I went in prison. Come Monday morning."

She swallowed hard. Two days to decide what to do. She could figure something out by then. She was sure she could. "All right."

"Promise?"

"I promise. You have to promise me you won't go near Dan or the kids until we talk again."

"'Kay." He sounded like Molly and Sara. "Kiss me goodbye."

Her stomach revolted at the thought. *Keep your cool, Tess.*

The best she could do was brush her lips over his forehead.

"WHERE'S MOM?" Sara stood in the doorway to the family room. She and Molly had been watching a video while Dan fixed lunch.

Frying bacon at the stove, Dan glanced to the clock. "She should be home any minute now."

She was an hour late. He'd tried to reach her on her cell phone, but she wasn't answering. Usually she was back in time for lunch on these Saturday mornings she took for herself. Maybe she'd decided to get a massage after yoga, although he didn't know why she'd pay for one. He'd be glad to take on the job himself—free of charge. And offer fringe benefits. He smiled.

"I'm hungry." Molly had joined her sister in the doorway. Her hair was up in a messy ponytail, and her shorts and shirt were already grimy.

"Okay, let's eat." He took the bacon out of the pan and placed it on paper towels to drain. "Mom can have a sandwich when she gets home."

They were halfway through BLT's when he heard the garage door go up.

"Mom's home!" Molly jumped up and headed to the kitchen door before it even opened.

Tessa stepped inside.

Molly stopped a foot from her mother. "Holy cow, Mommy, what happened?"

Sara gasped, her mouth open.

"Oh, Lord, Tessa." Dan rushed to her.

She looked awful. Her eyes were frantic and her face pale. Except for a huge bruise spreading from her nose across her left cheek. "Sweetheart, what happened?"

Her hand went to her face and she winced. "It's not as bad as it looks."

He doubted that. But Tessa downplayed any

injury or illness, and he knew she wouldn't want to alarm the kids any more than she already had.

"Mommy, who *hit* you?"

She swayed on her feet and reached out for purchase.

Dan grabbed for her arm. "Here, girls, let me get Mom seated." As he led her to a chair, he felt her trembling. "Easy, love."

"Mommy, I asked you a question."

"Nobody hit me, honey. Why would you ask that?"

"Peter's father hit him twice and his face looked like that."

Tessa frowned. "I didn't know Peter's father hit him."

"He doesn't live with Peter anymore."

His pulse still tripping, Dan sat beside her. "What happened?"

"You know how clumsy I can be. I came down the loft stairs too fast after yoga, and I lost my footing. I fell and hit my face on the iron handrail."

His youngest shook her head. "You're not clumsy. Daddy says you're as graceful as a gaz—" Sara looked at him. "What, Dad?"

"A gazelle. You are. I can't believe you fell."

She shrugged. "I guess I was still in that trance-like state meditating creates." She tried to joke. "They call it woo-woo land."

"Did François call the paramedics?"

"No, no. Everyone at The Yoga Experience is

trained in first aid and CPR. We iced my cheek, off and on. They wouldn't let me drive until they were sure I was clearheaded. I guess that's why I'm so late."

This late? But she looked as if she was ready to collapse, so Dan didn't push it. "Does it need more ice?"

Her fingertips traced the bruise. She was still shaking. "I think so."

"Let's get you upstairs so you can lie down." He turned to his daughter. "Molly, get the ice bag out of the laundry room, fill it and bring it up to our bedroom."

"No, Dan, finish eating."

"You're kidding, right?"

"I—" she studied his face "—I guess I'm not thinking straight."

"Come on." He helped her stand and she leaned on him all the way up the steps.

In the bedroom, he helped her stretch out, removed her sneakers and, when the girls brought the ice, he placed it on her cheek. Despite Tessa's protestations, he sent the kids downstairs.

"I'm sorry to cause such a fuss."

He struggled to rein in his temper, which was taking precedence over his fear. "I wish you'd caused more."

Her head on the pillow, she gazed up at him. "What?"

He didn't say anything.

"You sound angry."

"No, honey, I'm worried. You should have called me. I can't believe you stayed there with strangers and then drove home by yourself. From the looks of you, you were in no condition to be behind the wheel, no matter what François decided."

She blew out a heavy breath. "I'm sorry. As I said, I wasn't thinking clearly."

Something was odd about all this. Tessa always called him when things went wrong. Hell, he called her, too, for even stupid little annoyances. They joked about their emotional codependence.

"No matter, now. At least you're here. Safe, where I can take care of you."

Her expression got bleak.

"Sweetheart, what is it?"

"Nothing. I need to rest."

"Then close your eyes."

She held tightly to his hand. "Don't leave yet."

"I won't, honey. I'll be here. Forever."

She must be more shaken than she let on. He held her hand until she fell into a fitful sleep. Dan watched her for a long time, unable to dismiss a sense of foreboding. Something else was going on here. Something was wrong with Tessa, and she wasn't telling him. Why?

CHAPTER SEVEN

MR. MOONEY, the manager of All State Bank, was a talker. Usually, Tessa didn't mind the older man tying her up when she did the banking; his wife Miriam had died two years ago, and he was lonely. She made a habit of building in an extra few minutes when she went, in case she bumped into him. But today, she had no time or energy to spare. She didn't want to talk to anybody. She wanted to crawl under the blankets in her safe bedroom, bury her head and forget the nightmare her life had become. In only two days, everything had changed. She could lose the life she had with Dan.

Mr. Mooney spotted her as soon as she entered the building. "Mrs. Logan, how nice to see—oh, dear, what happened to your cheek?"

The bruises had turned from purple to red to yellow and were still noticeable. "I fell at yoga class on Saturday."

His eyes, muddy with age, brightened. "Miriam took yoga. The back-care class."

"Yes, I knew that. She loved it, Mr. Mooney."

"I'm sorry you were hurt. Is your cheek still sore today?"

"A bit. It looks worse than it is."

He glanced over at the counters. "Here, let me escort you to a line."

"No, please, don't bother."

"I'll keep you company. There are only two tellers on, as of yet. There are more customers than we expected at 9:00 a.m."

Like a courtly gentleman, he stood with her, chatting about his garden and what annuals he'd put in over Memorial Day. How it was hard to plant the bulbs these days because of his knee, which he'd injured when he was a medic in Vietnam.

She realized he had asked her a question. "I'm sorry, what did you say?"

"I was inquiring about your family."

"Fine. They're fine."

Thankfully she reached the head of the queue, and Mr. Mooney left her to do her business. She wouldn't want him to see that she was withdrawing a lot of cash.

The teller was new. "Can I help you?"

"I'd like five thousand dollars from this account." Her own personal one. Dan had no access to this money. On occasion, he'd asked her how much she had in there, and every April he needed to know for tax purposes. She thought of the overnight at the bed and breakfast they were planning for this weekend. Would she still have enough to pay for that? Just barely.

Please God, let us still be taking that trip. For two days, she'd been hit with those kinds of thoughts, which often led to panic attacks. What would happen if Dan found out about her past, despite her best efforts to make Frankie leave her alone? Would her husband still love her?

"Mrs. Logan? How do you want the money?"

"In a cashier's check." She gave Frankie's name.

Mr. Mooney caught up with her after she completed her transaction. They chatted another few minutes, then said goodbye.

Out in the bright morning light, Tessa put on her sunglasses, turned left and bumped right in to someone. They both stumbled back. "Oh, excuse me."

The woman righted herself and frowned. It took Tessa a minute to realize the glare wasn't because they'd collided. A smooth, cultured voice said, "Hello, Tessa."

"Hello, Allison." Dan's old girlfriend. "How have you been?"

"Well." She studied Tessa's face. "You've looked better."

She touched her cheek. "I know." Dan should have married this prep-schooled, Harvard-educated, well-dressed woman. No. Tessa had garnered enough self-esteem to get over that feeling long ago, but with Frankie's return... "I was sorry to hear about your divorce, Allison."

Allison's gray eyes clouded. "Yes, well, we can't all marry men like Dan."

"Allison, I—"

"Never mind. I shouldn't have said that." Her confidence showed signs of strain. "I'm still raw from the breakup. It was only nine months ago."

"I'm sorry."

"Because I know you really mean that, I'll apologize for being snotty. I know you and Dan have a solid marriage and a happy life." She straightened her shoulders and all traces of vulnerability fled. "I need to get into the bank."

Tessa watched the woman go inside the big, modern building. She couldn't expend any energy on Allison, either. She had more pressing problems. What was she going to do if the bribe she had in her purse didn't work? She had to make it work. She had to.

Frankie Hamilton was a sick man. She'd gone online yesterday and looked up his symptoms. He vacillated between reality and a dream world, in which Tessa wrote him letters and asked him to come to her rescue. He had an insane jealousy where Tessa was concerned. He thought someone loved him who didn't. Frankie had had the same symptoms when he was young, except for the latter, because Tessa *had* been in love with him. His paranoia and feelings of persecution had dominated then. People in town had branded him crazy for as long as she could remember. The M.D. Web site she'd consulted labeled his condition a delusional disorder. The notion made her panic. Who knew what a crazy man could do?

Briefly, she'd considered calling the police and having Frankie arrested for assault. But then it would come out publicly about her past with the man. Dan would be humiliated in front of the whole community and his reputation ruined. There had to be another way.

Forcing herself not to break down, she crossed the street and, instead of going to her car, circled to the hotel. Dark from the shade of the other buildings, the alley snaked behind the businesses downtown and—lucky for her—there was a back door to the Heritage House. Just before she went inside, she wrapped a scarf around her head and pushed up her sunglasses. She felt like an idiot from one of those grade B movies. Still, she'd do what she had to do to protect her family, without ruining Dan's reputation.

DAN WAS IN THE conference room of the Public Safety Building, trying to concentrate on what his assistant D.A. was saying, but his professional focus was shot to hell. He couldn't stop thinking about the bruise on Tessa's face. And the fact that, as Molly had noted, it looked as if someone had slapped her. Logically, he knew that was next to impossible. With the exception of maybe Allison, his wife didn't have one single enemy. No one would wish her ill will, let alone do her physical harm.

"Dan? I asked you a question."

"Sorry, Karen. Ask again."

"Do you want the stalker case, or should I take it?"

"Fill me in on it. Then we'll decide."

"Harriet Phelps was arrested for stalking. The inciting incident was when she shoved her ex's new girlfriend around in the parking garage downtown."

"Was the woman hurt?"

"Broke an ankle. Harriet's a big girl. There were previous incidents of harassment. The girlfriend recognizes now that she should have reported them to the police."

"So we have no paper trail."

"None. But there was a witness to the assault in the garage. And they have an answering machine tape of threatening calls."

"That should be enough to make some headway. Go ahead and take it, if you want."

His assistant shifted in her seat. "Actually, I don't want it. I, um, had a stalker in college. It was an unpleasant experience."

"Karen, I'm sorry. I didn't know. Were you hurt?"

"Roughed up somewhat. The guy ended up doing jail time. My father went ballistic, which was the worst thing."

"I can't imagine what I'd do if someone threatened my family. Of course, I'll take the case."

"I didn't want you to have to handle this one."

"Why?"

"Allison Markham is the defense attorney." She shrugged. "That woman doesn't make things easy for you."

The legal world in Orchard Place was small. "It's no big deal."

"Allison's due here in an hour."

Dan returned to his office annoyed that he had to see Allison on top of everything else. He picked up his phone and punched in Tess's number. No answer. Why? She had planned to stay home today. And she was sore, so she'd canceled walking with Janey this morning. He tried her cell, but she didn't pick up. Leaving a brief message, he clicked off. It was stupid to be worried about where she was.

He'd about convinced himself he was being overprotective—hadn't he and Tessa just fought about that trait—when Allison walked into his office.

"We meet again," she said, rolling her eyes.

"Defense attorneys and D.A.s usually do, Allison. Have a seat."

As she dropped into a chair in front of his desk, she asked, "What's wrong with Tessa? She looks terrible."

"Excuse me?"

"I saw Tessa coming out of the bank this morning. She looks like she had a run-in with a Mack truck."

Why the hell would his wife be at the bank early this morning? She always did the banking at the end of the week. He glanced at the phone. And where the hell was she now?

SMILING AT HIMSELF in the mirror, Frankie combed back his hair, then applied the new aftershave he had bought at the drugstore this morning. Trixie always liked cologne on him. He was a little nervous and wanted to look his best when he saw her in a few minutes.

She'd called him late last night.

I love you, Frankie. Don't listen to what I say about those other people, about that guy Dan and his daughters. I get confused sometimes, and I don't mean any of it. Please, take me away from all this. I'll bring the money so you can get your car. We'll go away in it.

A knock.

Reassured he looked good in a denim shirt and clean jeans, he took a swig of the cough medicine he'd bought along with the cologne then opened the door. He frowned when he saw her. "What happened to your face, baby?"

Her eyes widened beneath the scarf she wore. "You…" She stopped. "I got hurt, Frankie."

"I'm so sorry." He thought hard. "Did that guy do this to you? If he did, I swear I'll kill him."

"No, no, I fell."

He saw a maid down the hall go into another room, and the door slammed. "Come inside."

Drawing in a breath—must be she was as nervous as him—she stepped into the room. Her back to him, she began rummaging around in her purse. He came up behind her, and placed his hands on her shoulders. She jumped.

"Easy."

He could hear her breath quicken.

"I know," he whispered in her ear. "I feel grateful that we're together, too." He bent to nuzzle her neck and her scent enveloped him. From the first day he'd met her, Trixie always smelled like fresh flowers that had been out in the rain.

She whirled, dislodging his hands. "Don't, Frankie."

That made him mad. "I don't understand you. I let it go last night, but, Trixie, I been down for fifteen years. I wanna have sex."

Backing up a step, she clutched her purse to her chest like a shield. "I can't have sex with you, Frankie."

"Why the hell not?"

"Because I'm married to another man."

"You don't love him. You told me last night."

"What?"

"You called at midnight after he was asleep. You said you didn't love him, any of them."

"Oh, Frankie, I didn't call you. I didn't say I don't love Dan. I do."

His head began to ache, and his vision blurred. He started coughing again. "No, you don't mean that. You're mine."

"Maybe I was once. That's what you're

confused about. But I'm not anymore. I belong with Dan and my girls."

"Then why are you here?"

She pulled something out of her purse. "I brought you a cashier's check for five thousand dollars. For the car you want. You can go away and get a new start."

He stared at the check. "You brought me money?"

"Yeah, Frankie. You're going to need it to go somewhere and get a job. Start a life."

"But I ain't goin' no place without you."

Her face flushed. She shoved the check out farther. "Take this, Frankie, you can't stay in Orchard Place."

"You're here."

"You can't have me."

"Trixie, I gotta have you. That's all I wanted for those fifteen stinkin' years in jail."

"No."

He grabbed her purse and it tipped to the side, spilling the contents. When he squatted to pick the stuff up, he found a picture. For a long time, he stared at it hard. Then, he stood, and very carefully, he tore a piece off. He handed the photo back. "You can bring them, I guess."

She looked down at the picture and gasped. "You can't remove Dan from my life because you want to, Frankie."

"Oh, yeah?" he said. "Wanna bet?"

Tessa gasped and wondered if she was going to be able to handle Frankie Hamilton.

DAN SLAMMED THE BALL into the front of the court. It bounced back like a bullet, and Nick had to jump out of the way to avoid getting hit. "My point."

"And my neck. Damn it, Dan, I want to be able to walk out of here."

Cocking his head, Dan stared at his brother. "Chicken shit."

Nick laughed. "You're on buddy. You aren't gonna know what hit you."

For a half hour they pummeled the ball, and by the time they were finished Dan had a floor burn on one knee and Nick had a bruise on his temple from where he'd banged into the wall. They were covered with sweat and were breathing hard. They crossed to their gym bags and got out their towels to wipe their faces.

"You gonna tell me about this?" Nick asked.

"About what?"

"Why you're playing like this was the Olympics of racquetball. You were a crazy man out there." He chuckled. "Not that it's a bad thing. About time you lost some of your legendary control."

"Don't start on me about that."

Serious now, Nick frowned. "Spit it out, Dan. You're not yourself today."

Dan hit the wall with his racquet, sending shooting pain up his arm. "Shit."

Nick was silent. Since he'd straightened out his

life, he'd become a sounding board, among other things.

"Something's going on with Tessa."

"Our Tessa?"

Leaning against the wall, Dan gave him a small smile. "Yeah, *our* Tessa."

"Physically?"

"Well, no, unless you count the bruise on her cheek." He shook his head. "Like somebody slapped her."

"Not you?"

His racket dropped to the floor, clattering on the wood. "Hell, no! How can you even ask me something like that?"

"Of course you wouldn't hurt her. I'm sorry."

"She said she fell onto a handrail at yoga. But that's not what it looks like. Besides, she was a basket case the rest of Saturday and all of yesterday."

"Why would she lie about how she got hurt?"

"I don't know."

"Did you ask her?"

"It's hard to call your wife a liar to her face."

"I guess."

There was pounding on the door to signal other players were ready for their allotted time. Dan and Nick left the court and stopped at a juice bar for some water.

Once seated, Dan picked up the conversation. "I can't fathom what's going on, Nick. Who on earth would ever hit my wife? And, as far as I know, we've never lied to each other."

"Dishonesty, your hot button."

"And she knows it. She promised she'd always be honest with me."

"Sometimes people need privacy, Dan."

"You'd defend her lying to me?"

"You don't know she's lying."

"It's a feeling. Based on gut instinct—damn it, I know my wife—and how she's always been about her past."

"The fact that she won't talk about it?"

"I have a basic outline of her life before she came here. But I have a bad feeling about what went on then." He waited. "What would you do if you were me?"

"If she were my wife, I'd probably do anything I had to in order to keep her happy."

"I do that, Nick. For most everything."

"I know you do. Give her some space. See what she comes up with on her own."

"Maybe."

Dan hated being a control freak. Maybe Nick was right. If something was wrong with Tessa, he'd rather she came to him and told him about it without his having to drag it out of her.

TESSA SAT ON A BENCH in the park waiting for Janey to show up for their walk. It promised to be a sparkling June day. She was so shaken, she had to dig her hands into her sweat suit jacket to keep them from trembling. Frankie was going to ruin her life, and there was nothing she could do about it. No, no, she wouldn't think that way. She had to be strong, to be the woman she'd become, not the girl she was when she'd known him.

Her sister jogged toward her wearing her hot-pink suit again. Tessa sat back in the shadow of the maple tree. By Tuesday morning, the bruises were pretty much gone, but Janey's protectiveness would kick in to high gear if she saw the remnants of Frankie's fist. On the phone on Sunday afternoon, Tessa had told Janey she'd gotten hurt, and Janey had wanted to come right over. Tessa persuaded her not to.

Janey sat next to Tessa on the bench. "Hi."

"Hi." Tessa nodded to the paper Janey held. "What's that?"

"I'm afraid to tell you."

"Is something wrong?" Tessa had been so self-absorbed, had something happened in her sister's life and she'd missed it?

"Yes. But not with me." She grabbed Tessa's hand. "For you, maybe."

"What?"

She held up the paper. "This is from the *Iverton Banner*."

"What are you doing with it?"

"I read it all the time. I like finding out what's happening in our hometown."

"I didn't know that."

"I thought it might upset you since your memories of Iverton are so bad."

"Yours aren't so great."

Janey shrugged and set the paper in her lap.

"What did you find that's upset you?"

"Frankie Hamilton was released from prison two weeks ago. I printed off a copy of the article for you."

Tessa looked away and said nothing.

"I know this is a shock. I guess it's about the right time for him to get out. But I wasn't expecting it. I wasn't even thinking about the creep, after you had your accident."

Tessa remained quiet.

"There's more."

Could Janey know something? It wasn't like her not to even inquire about the bruises. What if Frankie had contacted her sister? Please, God, no. The last thing she wanted was for Janey to be dragged in to this mess. Janey would be outraged, and tell Brad, or maybe even Dan. Tessa *had* to handle Frankie's return by herself. "More?"

"Oh, honey, the woman who was killed..."

"Serena Summers. And her five-year-old daughter, Joanna."

"Uh-huh. Ike Summers, the father, is quoted in

here about Frankie's release. He says Frankie should be locked up and the key thrown away."

"Just Frankie?"

Janey didn't answer.

"He said me, too, right? I should be locked up forever."

"I'm sorry, Tess."

She swallowed back her revulsion, felt her self-esteem crumble. Obscene images of the car wreck and the people who were killed forced their way into her consciousness. "Me, too. You don't know how sorry."

"I knew you'd take this hard." When Tessa didn't comment, Janey added, "But, Tess, nothing's different. I told you because…"

Her head snapped up. "What?"

"Frankie was obsessed with you. Do you remember what he said after your trial?"

She shook her head, but she'd never forget what he'd screamed at her. He'd been a wild man and had to be restrained by the court officers. *I'll find you, baby, no matter what, I'll find you!*

"I'm afraid he's going to come looking for you, Tessa. Really afraid."

CHAPTER EIGHT

"COME ON, SARA, let me lift you up."

Tessa smiled over at her daughter, who Chelsea Chamberlain had grabbed under the arms and set on a stool. It was the morning of the Orchard Place Elementary School carnival, held at the end of each school year to raise money for a local charity or organization. All the parents volunteered, and Tessa was manning the fried dough booth. Chelsea, who was here because the money was going to the teen center, had asked to work with her and was showing Sara how to use the sifter to put powdered sugar on the dough. They both had some of the confection on their hair and faces.

The second week of June was warm, and Tessa was sweating. Her stomach felt queasy, too, from the constant smell of grease. She didn't care, though. She wanted to do something constructive. Her week had been filled with frustration and petrifying worry.

First, she'd lied to her sister Wednesday morning in the park. *No, nothing's wrong. Just the thought of*

Frankie upsets me. But I don't think he'll come here. How could he find me, anyway?

Since Janey knew her so well, she'd looked unconvinced. *You should tell Dan about your past. In case anything happens.*

Maybe.

Tessa tried to quell her anxiety and concentrate on the pieces of dough she lifted out of the fryer with a slotted spoon, but she was afraid she was going to have to tell Dan about Frankie. The situation was deteriorating fast. She'd been so sure she could make him leave, she'd believed Frankie would be gone by now and everybody would be safe. But he wasn't gone. And his delusions had gotten more pronounced. And after she'd realized Frankie was the guy Dan and Molly met in the park, Tessa agonized that she could be endangering her children. If he hadn't gotten sick, she'd be at the crossroads of this thing already.

But he'd come down with a bad case of the flu with severe cold symptoms and had taken to bed with it. Tessa had brought him medicine and one of those plug-in vaporizers to alleviate his symptoms. She had always felt sorry for Frankie when he was ill and that hadn't changed.

"Hey, pretty lady, ready for a break?" She glanced over her shoulder to find Dan standing at her booth. He'd volunteered for the basketball throw with Molly.

She studied her husband. The sun glinted off his dark hair, highlighting a few strands of gray that weren't normally visible. Despite that, he seemed fit and youthful in his dark green shorts and green tee. He was smiling at her affectionately.

"I don't have anyone to relieve me."

"Go ahead," Chelsea said. "Sara and I can hold down the fort back here. I got her trained on how to do the sugar."

"See, Daddy?" Sara held up the sieve. Some sugar sifted from the stainless steel instrument into her lap.

"Great job, princess."

Mavis, the woman at the cash register, agreed. "Tessa, you've been slaving over that hot fryer long enough. Go for a break. You look a little peaked."

Coward that she was, she didn't want to be with Dan. Every time they were alone, she was afraid he'd question her about her bruises again or why she was behaving so oddly. Tessa had tried to rein in her reactions but wasn't always successful. She'd snapped at him when he asked her about her bank visit early in the week. She was on the edge. She was already dreading the trip they were taking right after the fair. Tonight they were going to a B&B in Geneva then heading to Rockford the next day so Dan could give a speech to the Rotary on stopping juvenile crime.

"Tessa?"

"All right. I do need a break. This grease is getting to me."

When she came out of the booth he said, "You do look a little worse for wear. We'll get something cold to drink."

Her hand went to her hair and she sighed. "I'm a mess."

"I like the curls."

"What?"

"Your hair. It's curling around your face and out of the ponytail. I told you before that I like it like that. I don't know why you straighten it all the time."

Because it belonged to the person I used to be.

"I'm too old to play Goldilocks."

"You still look like a kid." He took her hand and they started to walk. "I like the pearls, too. Though you don't usually wear them with casual clothes."

She fingered the precious gift. Frankie had used the money she'd brought to pay a week's hotel bill and buy a used car—which had sat in the parking lot since he was ill. They needed more money, he'd said, so they could have something to live on when they left town. Though she reiterated that she wasn't going with him, he'd told her to get the damn cash. Since she only had enough in her account for this weekend's getaway, she had to have another way to come up with money to placate him. The thought of selling the pearls broke her heart.

"You okay?" Dan asked. "You got quiet."

"Just enjoying the scenery." They walked through the grounds, which were set up with a Ferris wheel, a mini roller coaster and several kiddie attractions. There were game booths—basketball shooting, ring toss, a duck draw for the little ones—scattered across the grounds in the back of the school.

They passed a face-painting booth, and Dan waved to Nick, who had taken Molly with him; she was getting some kind of emblem on her face. One of Nick's kids, Beth, was doing the painting and making Molly laugh. The childlike sound drifted over to them.

"You doing all right?" he asked, giving his attention back to Tessa.

Here it comes. "Fine."

"You've been on edge all week."

"Have I?"

"Hmm." He nodded. "I'm really glad we're getting away tonight. We can rest and relax. Talk some."

"It's nice of your mother to pick up the girls and take them to the festival in Naples for an overnight." At least they'd be safe from Frankie while she and Dan headed out to the Finger Lakes, or she never would have left them.

"Are you looking forward to seeing Jay?" His law school roommate had set up the presentation.

"Not as much as I'm looking forward to being alone with my wife."

They reached the drink stand. "Get a seat and I'll bring us lemonade."

Tessa found some shade and tried to calm her stomach. How could she hold Dan off? She watched him smile at the concession stand worker, pay for the lemonade and speak to someone next to him. She loved him so much and just wanted his arms around her.

How come you won't let me near you, Trixie?

Early in the week Frankie had tried to get physical with her. He'd backed off when he'd taken ill. But she knew the advances would resume soon. Just the thought of another man touching her made her ill. She belonged to Dan, physically and emotionally.

"Here you go," Dan said, setting down drinks, smiling at her. "Relax and enjoy it."

As she sipped her lemonade, she studied him. She knew him so well. *He* knew something was wrong with her, and he was trying to hide his concern. "Dan, I'm fine. First the fall, and I'll be getting my period in a few days. I'm always shaky and out of sorts during this time of the month, you know that."

"I know what you're like then, honey. But this is different."

"Dan? Hello."

They looked up to see Mitch Nash at their table. Tall, trim and fit for over sixty, he'd been mayor of Orchard Place for ten years. Several times, he'd tried to recruit Dan to work on his staff and perhaps pursue a career in politics, but Dan had refused.

"Hi, Mitch."

Tessa smiled. "Mitch."

Gesturing to the grounds, his smile was that of a proud grandfather's. "The fair's great again this year."

"It always is," Dan said.

"You chaired it for two years in a row, didn't you, Tessa?"

"Yes. It's a lot of work. This year's committee did a terrific job."

"Your grandchildren go here, don't they?" Dan asked.

"Yes. But I would have come anyway to support the cause. Money's going to the center where your brother works. I hear he's doing wonders there. You two were obviously cut from the same cloth."

Dan's jaw tensed. He and Nick had got close in the two years Nick had been back, but his unsavory past still rankled Dan. Oh, God, if he was angry or embarrassed by what his brother had done, what would he feel about *her* if he found out?

"So, we're all set for Tuesday night, right?"

"Yes."

"We're thrilled about Dan's honor," Tessa said.

"I assume the whole family will be there."

"All except my brother-in-law, Brad Christopher. He's in London and won't be able to get back."

"And your mother, Dan? Will she be there?"

"With bells on."

"I'm glad to hear that."

The mayor left, and Tessa smiled after him. "I think Mitch has a crush on Claire."

The lemonade glass stopped halfway to Dan's lips. "*That* would be political suicide."

"What do you mean?"

His eyes hardened. "My father was a criminal, Tessa. By association, my mother's reputation is tainted. People around here still remember what happened."

"Dan, that was twenty-five years ago."

"These things follow you. You can never completely escape them. It's one of the reasons I'm not going into politics. I can't afford to have my past scrutinized."

"But that's ridiculous. You and your mother did nothing wrong."

"Nick thinks she knew something was going on."

"Nick can't see straight where your mother's concerned."

"I know. I've talked to him about it, but he won't budge."

"I'm surprised he even came back to Orchard Place."

"It was because of me, and I'm damned glad he did." Dan angled his head. "Listen, how did we get on to this? I hate talking about my father."

"I don't know. I'm sorry it upsets you so much."

He shrugged. "I've spent my adult life trying to overcome the stigma my father left us with. I know it's made me obsessive. I try not to be that way, but the feelings are there, Tess, and I can't do anything about them."

Emotion churned inside her. She was going to lose him, if Frankie told him about her.

Dan's jaw was rigid and his shoulders tense. Tessa reached over and squeezed his free hand. "You're doing just fine, Mr. Citizen of the Year."

He held on to her. "Thanks, sweetheart."

"For what?"

"Accepting me, flaws and all. I wish I was more like you."

Oh, Lord.

"Mom! Dad!" Glad for the interruption, Tessa glanced up as Molly dragged Nick toward them. "Look, I got my face painted. It's mad-cool." On her right cheek was a miniature devil.

"Nick, you let her get that?" Tessa asked.

"Appropriate, I think."

Tessa's eyes narrowed on her daughter. "Why?"

Pretending interest in her sneakers, Molly mumbled, "No reason."

"Tell your mother what you did at the duck draw," Dan said.

Her daughter shook her head.

"When no one was looking…" Dan told her "…Molly let the water out."

"Molly, what are we going to do with you?"

"I was playing around. I was only gonna let a little out, but it came real fast." She tugged on Nick's hand. "Come over here. I wanna go on the Ferris wheel. Beth said she'd take a break and go with us."

"See ya," Nick said and headed off with Molly.

Dan watched them go. "Little Miss Mischief. I hope she outgrows it."

Tessa had taken a sip of the tart lemonade and choked on it.

"You okay?"

"Fine."

But she wasn't, and she didn't know if she'd ever be again.

Especially when she saw a familiar figure lurking behind the lemonade stand.

FRANKIE HAD ABOUT had it with waiting. He felt better this morning and went to find Trixie. It wasn't hard. He knew about her kids with that other guy—though sometimes he forgot about them—and he saw a poster advertising this carnival, so he bet she'd be here. Just as he was going to confront her and the guy, they stood to leave. When she veered off alone, he followed her. He needed to get a few things straight and to show her who was boss. For a minute, he felt bad about doing that. She'd nursed him all week when he was sick, just like she used to do all those years ago. But she hadn't said she'd leave with him, and something had to give.

He was waiting behind a tent right next to where Tessa was working, trying to decide how to get

Trixie out of there, when a woman came toward her booth. Furious, he stepped out from the shadows and headed her off.

"If it ain't Miss High and Mighty."

Janey jumped back, her hand to her heart, her mouth dropping open. Then, an expression of such revulsion came over her face, he wanted to smack her. His hand fisted and he took a step toward her.

She paled, which made him feel big. And powerful. Looming over her, he said, "How've you been, Sister Janey?"

"What are you *doing* here?"

He angled his head toward the fried dough booth, and she tracked his gaze.

"Oh, no, Frankie, you can't. Please, don't let Tessa know you're in town."

"You think you know so much. You think you got power over her life? I do. Not you. She always did tell me more than you."

"What does that mean?

"Take a wild guess."

Janey's eyes widened. "She knows you're in town. You've already seen her?"

"More than that." He leered at her sister. "A lot more."

"I don't believe it."

"She didn't tell you I was in town, did she?"

"No. How long have you been here?"

"A couple of weeks."

"Oh, Lord, no."

"Don't talk about the Lord."

"I'm sure He gave up on you a long time ago."

Frankie hated hearing that. His father used to say God didn't create stupid heads in His image. But in prison, Frankie had gone to Bible study and Chaplain Cook said God would like and forgive him if he repented his sins.

"Shut up. Or I'll have to hurt you."

Janey drew herself up to her whole five-foot-four height. "Frankie, what do you want? Money? I'll give you some."

"Trixie already gave me that and more, if you get my drift."

"I think I'm going to be sick."

"Screw you," Frankie said. "She loves me and I'm takin' her away from here. She even bought us a car, which is proof that she wants to leave this hick town." As soon as he said it, he knew it was the truth. Of course she wanted to leave with him.

"You're crazy."

His head swam and he grabbed Janey's arms and shook her. Jarred by the movement, her teeth clacked together.

"Don't say that." He shook her harder. "I hate when people say that to me."

"Let her go, Frankie."

They both turned to find Trixie standing a few

feet away. "Janey," she said calmly. "Get away from here now."

Janey freed herself from Frankie and flew to Trixie's side. "Come with me. We'll go get Dan. And Nick. They can help us."

Trixie shook her head. Her curls were back, a sign that she was her old self again. "No, nobody can help me." She faced her sister. "Meet me back at my booth in a half hour. We'll talk then."

Janey looked horrified. "I'm not leaving you alone with this lunatic."

Frankie took a step forward, planning to silence the bitch once and for all. Trixie stepped between them.

"I'll be fine. I'm handling this. We'll talk later." When Janey still didn't move, Trixie's voice got all shaky. "Please, Janey, do this for me."

"All right."

"And promise me you won't tell anybody about Frankie. Not Dan."

"No, I won't promise that."

Her eyes got tears in them. Damn her sister for making her sad. "Janey, please. Not until we talk."

After a long hesitation, Janey agreed. "All right, I promise. I hate you." she spat at Frankie. "I wish they'd put you on death row for what you did and what you are." With that she walked away.

Fury bubbled inside him and he grabbed Trixie's arm a lot harder than he meant to. These people kept making him *do* things. "You're coming with me."

"No, Frankie, wait."

"I'm done waitin'."

He dragged her toward the parking lot.

TERRIFIED, Tessa let herself be shoved into the front seat of Frankie's car. It was all going to come out now, she knew it, and she wouldn't be able to do anything about it. She felt immobilized, like she used to when she was a kid and Frankie took over.

The only thing she had to be thankful for was that the nondescript sedan was in a shaded spot and no one was around. Frankie got into the driver's side and went to start the engine, but she stayed his hand. God, she hated touching him. "Frankie, wait, please."

"Why?"

"I have responsibilities here."

"Screw them. I'm takin' you away."

In a desperate attempt to halt this madness, she said, "All right. I'll go away with you. But not until next week."

"Hell, why not till then?"

"For one thing, I've got to get us more money." She touched the pearls that caressed her neck. "I'll have to hock these. For another, I can't disappear. Dan will call the cops." When he looked unconvinced, she had a brainstorm. "I'm also scheduled to go on a church retreat. I'm leaving tonight, as a matter of fact. I'll be back Tuesday."

He shook his head. "No."

"I'm the lay leader for some workshops and if I don't show up, it will cause a big stir."

He studied her. *Please, God, don't let him know I'm lying.*

"You didn't tell me that before. About church. I don't like messing with church stuff. God might get mad at me again."

Bingo.

"Oh, Frankie, God really wants me to do this. God will be angry at us both if I don't go."

He massaged his temples. Tessa noticed he did that when his delusions came, or when he got confused.

"Let's do this right, Frankie, and no one will stop us."

"I guess that's okay. But Tuesday. No later."

"Tuesday. I promise." She willed back her disgust, her stomach roiling. "Now, you need to go back to the hotel. I'll see you Tuesday morning and we can make plans."

"We're leavin' next week, right?" Once again, he reminded her of her kids, always asking for reassurance. When he got like that, she felt sorry for him. In some ways he was a child.

"Yes."

"Okay."

"I've got to get to my booth before anybody misses me." She reached for the handle of the door.

His hand closed around her like a vise. "Not so fast. I need somethin'."

"W-what?"

"A kiss. To tide me over. And when you get back, we ain't gonna wait till we leave. We're gonna have sex right away."

Oh, God, no. "I can't kiss you here. It's broad daylight. Somebody might see us."

"Like I care."

"I care."

"Tough shit. I want a kiss or I'm gonna go find that guy Logan and tell him about us. To hell with your retreat."

Tessa started to tremble.

He smiled at her. "I know, baby, me, too. I miss us, too." He yanked on her arm and pulled her as close as the gear shift would allow. She felt her stomach contract as he lowered his head.

MINUTES LATER, Tessa stumbled out of the car.

She was breathing so fast she was afraid she was going to hyperventilate. She wanted a shower. She wanted to die. But she had to be strong, had to get through this. She *could* get through this. She'd endured almost two years in prison, had two difficult childbirths and had lived in fear for ten years that she was going to be exposed. She had to hold on.

Take one day at a time. Get through today and worry about next week later, worry about Frankie later.

Frankie.

And an ugly kiss. An obscene, sickening kiss.

She hurried behind some trees off to the side of the parking lot, dropped to her knees and wretched. She was a horrible person, and deserved all this. She'd made no progress from who she was when Frankie ran their car into that poor woman and her daughter. Her head splitting, she was hot all over as she continued to throw up.

She didn't know how long it had been when she heard, "Tessa? My God, are you all right?"

She looked up. The bright sunlight blinded her for a minute, and she saw only the figure of a man. Then she realized her brother-in-law, Nick, was standing over her. He squatted down and placed a hand on her shoulder. "You're sick."

She nodded.

"Are you done?"

His tone was concerned. Again, she nodded. He gave her his handkerchief, and she wiped her face as best she could.

"Can I help you up?"

"I guess." She tried to stand. "How did you…?" But she lost her balance and grabbed Nick for support.

He held her close for a minute. "Find you?"

"Uh-huh."

"Honey, you left your booth without telling anyone and never came back. Chelsea found me. Dan's frantic. We've been searching all over for you. I said I'd check the parking lot."

Oh, God, Nick could have happened upon her sooner. Or Dan might have come to the parking lot himself and seen her in the car. The man she loved could have witnessed that sleazy scene in the car.

The thought was enough to drive her to her knees again.

CHAPTER NINE

AT SEVEN THAT NIGHT, Dan and Tessa were shown to their second-floor suite at Belhurst Castle in Geneva, a huge stone building with turrets and peaked roofs that was at one time a real castle. It had been renovated into a rustic inn with all the modern amenities.

Tessa had slept the entire ninety-minute drive up to the Finger Lakes, so Dan had no answers as to what had happened at the fair. Yet. But that was going to change right now. After the bellman deposited their bags and left, Tessa crossed the plank wood floor to their suitcase, unzipped it and began removing their belongings.

Coming up behind her, Dan put his hands on her shoulders. "Stop unpacking, Tess. We have to talk. I'm worried about you, and I want some answers."

Her hands clutched at the dress she'd brought for dinner tonight. Not a good sign. "About what?"

He tugged her around to face him. "You're kidding, right?"

Her face was blank.

"About what happened today at the fair."

She huffed out an impatient sigh. "I wasn't feeling well. I told you that the heat combined with the greasy smell of the oil was making me ill. I thought I was going to be sick to my stomach, so I left."

"And went to the parking lot to get sick? I don't think so."

"After I got away from the fryer, I thought some fresh air and sunshine would make me feel better, so I went for a walk. But when I reached the parking lot, it got worse."

"Why would you leave without telling anyone?"

"You don't think clearly when you're ready to toss your cookies, Dan."

"Why—"

"Stop it!" Her voice rose. "I'm not one of your clients. I'm not on trial. Stop treating me that way."

Dan and Tessa almost never yelled at each other, so her outburst stunned him into silence. He stared at her, wondering where this stranger had come from, the one who had emerged from inside his even-tempered, sensitive wife.

Dropping his hands from her shoulders, he stood back. "Well, excuse me for worrying about the person I love most in the world." He grabbed the jacket he'd thrown on the bed. "I'm going out for a while."

She didn't try to stop him.

He hiked the grounds twice. The fact that it started

to drizzle helped cool him down. He hated when things were out of control like this. He liked his stable, ordinary life, the way it had been only a month ago. But more so, he didn't know how to fix things for Tessa if she refused to talk about what was bothering her. And no matter what she said, he was certain she was upset by something. Maybe he could talk to Janey when he got back. Or to Nick.

Hell. The only person it would help to talk to was Tessa. So what was he doing out here? He glanced at his watch. They had a dinner reservation at nine. The restaurant downstairs at the Castle was famous in the area, and they'd both been looking forward to it, as well as having a night alone. He smiled. The last time he'd brought her here, Sara had been conceived. With that happy memory, he jogged back to the inn.

The room was dim when he let himself in. Tessa was sitting in a chair overlooking the extensive grounds and the lake beyond them. She didn't turn when he shut the door. Or say anything. He shrugged out of his jacket and crossed to her. He was surprised to see she held a glass of wine and caught sight of an open bottle on the table, which had been in the gift basket in their room. He waited next to the chair but, still, she didn't speak, didn't look up at him.

"I'm sorry," he finally said. "I didn't realize my over-protectiveness was so bad."

Nothing. Instead, she curled her legs beneath her

and continued to sip the wine. Hell. What was this? She never gave him the cold shoulder, never froze him out. He moved in closer. She'd obviously showered. Her hair was curling around her face, and he could smell the scent of lotion. He noticed she wore satiny red pajamas. Looked like dinner was off.

He knelt down. "Sweetheart, look at me." When she did, he said what was in his heart. "I didn't know I was making you so unhappy."

Her eyes narrowed on him, and the accusation in them made him shiver in his damp clothes. "The only thing about you that makes me unhappy is when you badger me."

"Do I badger you?"

Giving him a withering look, she turned back to stare out the window. Again, she sipped her wine.

He remembered, then. A young Tessa, working at the diner. He'd systematically gone after her with all he'd had…

Please, one date. I know you like me.

A month later. *A kiss, Tessa. I can't wait to taste you.*

Six months later, drawing her to bed. *It's time for this, love.*

And finally: *You're pregnant? Hallelujah. Now you* have *to marry me.*

His voice was ragged when he said, "I've badgered you since we met, haven't I?"

"Yes." She looked back at him. "I love you, Dan,

more than I can express most of the time. And I'm glad we're married. But you lapse into this kind of thing and it hurts."

"Hurts?" He took her hand and kissed it. "I can't bear the thought of hurting you."

"I'm not sure you can stop."

"Of course I can. If you promise me you're not keeping something from me, that nothing's really wrong, I'll stop."

She swallowed hard. "I promise."

"All right, then." He brought her hand to his cheek and rested it there. His own fingers shaky, he outlined the low-cut neckline of the pajamas. She wore her pearls. The sight of them with slinky nightwear aroused him. His voice was husky when he said, "We're supposed to go to dinner."

"Forget dinner." Leaning over, she put the glass on the table, and stood. Drawing him up by the hand, she said, "Make love to me. Like you never have before. Please."

Because he'd promised, he ignored the desperation in her voice.

KNOWING THIS MIGHT BE the last time he touched her, Tessa blanked her mind and let herself go. His hand was big and firm and a bit calloused from working in the yard. And safe, she thought as she led him to the bed. Without haste, she unbuttoned his shirt and spread it open. She kissed the skin she bared. He smelled like clean rain and sweat.

"I should take a shower," he mumbled, his voice gruff, his hand on her neck.

"No, I don't want you to leave. And don't talk. Just feel."

She explored all the contours of his heated skin, relearning every dip and bulge of his muscles. His belt buckle stuck, and she yanked at it with two hands. His zipper whispered down. She pushed on his jeans and shorts and they slid to the floor. Then she pressed on his shoulders, urging him to sit on the bed. When he did, she knelt before him, removed his socks, shoes and the puddle of clothes.

He tunneled his hands through her hair. "Tessa, love…"

"Shh." Rising to her feet, she began to unfasten her pajamas. As she did, she watched him harden even more, took pleasure at the sight. She wanted him so aroused he'd forget everything. The satin slid off one shoulder. Then the other. Then the top was gone. She inched her fingers into her waistband and took her time sliding the garment down her hips. When she stepped out of them, Dan held on to her. Pulled her close. Buried his face in her stomach. Kissed her there.

After a few glorious moments, she dropped to her knees again. He gasped when she buried her face in his groin. Took him in her mouth. Rubbed up and down. They didn't do this often.

He braced his hands behind him, on the bed, and his head fell back. His moans were a blissful chorus, his hard breathing a joyful accompaniment.

Too soon, he sat up and pulled her to the bed. His face was flushed, his eyes wild as he covered her with his body. His mouth closed over hers, devoured her lips, her breasts. She kissed him back with a passion so great, a love so deep, she thought she might burst with it.

Within minutes, he parted her legs and thrust inside her. Hard. He drew back, almost out, then plunged again. Tessa grasped his shoulders when on the third thrust her body coiled, exploded. Almost simultaneously, Dan cried out and emptied himself in her.

His weight was heavy when he collapsed on top of her, his body slick with sweat. After a long while, he braced his forearms on the bed and lifted himself off her. Staring down, he brushed the hair out of her eyes. "Tess, love…"

She touched his mouth. "Shh. No talk."

"No talk?"

"Please, just hold me."

His expression puzzled, he rolled off her, and when he stretched out and drew her close, she could feel the tension returning to his body. She closed her eyes, and, in the safety of his arms, in minutes she drifted off.

ON THE MORNING of Dan's Citizen of the Year dinner, Tessa drove out of town. Glancing at the box on the seat next to her, she strengthened her resolve and headed for the Riverside Pawn Shop in Niagara Falls. She'd only survived the past few days because she'd blanked her mind. Otherwise, Tessa wouldn't have been able to do what she had to do.

A bridge loomed up ahead. For all her adult life, she'd hated to drive over the huge steel and concrete structures. She was always afraid she'd veer off right into the water or the highway beneath an overpass. Now, other more pressing fears superseded those, and she approached the bridge with resignation.

She'd managed to sidetrack Dan with sex most of the weekend. Along with unfair accusations. The latter made her ill—she'd manipulated him by going on the offense. She didn't regret the sex. It was wild and wonderful and brought them to a plane of raw intimacy.

After today, he'd never touch her again, no matter which way things went.

Tessa had made a plan. She wasn't going to leave town with Frankie. The notion was absurd. He was mentally unbalanced and she was afraid of him. But she was giving herself one more chance to convince him to leave her and her family alone. At the very least, she could buy time until after the awards dinner tonight. First, she'd give Frankie the money she was about to get and try to convince him to start a new life with it, without her. If that didn't work this time, either—which it probably wouldn't—there

was one recourse left. She was either going to have
to have sex with him, or he was going to tell Dan
about her past. Maybe by being with him, as revolt-
ing as that notion was, she could hold more sway
over him to make him leave town. He'd always been
nicer after sex.

Maybe not. He'd been suspicious when she'd
told him she was participating in a church retreat
this past weekend. He'd gone to see Janey at her
house. Janey had told her about it when she got
back from Rockford…

"Tessa, he was like a madman. He threatened me."

"Oh, Janey, I'm sorry."

"Thank God Brad was still away. Did you tell
him you were going away on a retreat?"

"I had to. I didn't know what else to say. He's got
this thing about offending God, and it seemed to work."

"What did Dan do when you told him about all
this?"

"I didn't tell him."

"What? When we talked at the fair before you left
for the Finger Lakes, you said you were going to do
it on the trip. While you had alone time together. He
could deal with your not telling him about your past
all these years."

"I'll explain it all tomorrow when we walk…"

Tessa found the pawn shop, a nondescript little
building in the heart of Niagara Falls, and parked in
the lot out front. It took only a few minutes to get rid

of her most precious possession, the pearls Dan had given her on their wedding day. She wanted to weep like a child at what she was doing, but she couldn't afford to be weak. So, with cold detachment, as if they were meaningless glass beads, she handed the beautiful strand over to the guy behind the counter, got the cash and the receipt and left the musty, chock-full-of-junk shop. She had one more thing to do before she went to see Frankie and give him the money.

It took her forty-five minutes to reach the center. She went in the old, brick, ivy-covered building and made her way to her brother-in-law's office on the first floor. He was seated behind his massive oak desk, talking on the phone. The space was wood paneled, and a wall of windows let in the natural light.

Nick hung up when she came in. "Hey, Tessa, how are you?"

"Fine. Chelsea isn't here yet?"

He glanced at his watch. "Any minute. She had a class until noon. We try to work around the kids' school schedule." He studied her, his gaze all too knowing. "Sit down."

Smoothing her hands over the plain black slacks she had put on this morning, she was vaguely surprised to see she wore a blouse Dan had bought her last year. "It's a positive sign that Chelsea wants to talk to me, isn't it, Nick?"

"Considering she's clammed up with everyone else, I think so."

"I'm glad I can help."

"Can I help you?"

Averting her gaze to a picture of the city on the wall, she pretended nonchalance. "What do you mean?"

"Don't BS me. Tessa. I know something's wrong with you and has been for a couple of weeks. I'm worried. About you and Dan."

"He's upset, I know."

"Talk to him."

She didn't respond.

"Then tell me what's going on. You don't have to be alone in whatever's happening to you."

Janey's exact sentiments. Dan's, too, indirectly. But Tessa wasn't going to include any of them in her deception. She'd handle this on her own, one way or another.

"All right, I admit, something's wrong. But I want to take care of it myself."

He cocked his head. "You know about my past, don't you?"

"I know you had it hard when your father left."

"Uh-huh. I turned into a juvenile delinquent, worse than my family knows, and Dan turned into Mr. Perfect."

"You've done a lot with your life. Don't diminish how far you've come."

"I don't. I've learned how to accept my mistakes and move on. But I know what it's like to have secrets. To be afraid because of them. Those feelings are all over your face these days. And truthfully, I've thought since the day I met you that you had wounds you weren't sharing with Dan. There's a kind of pervasive sadness about you, Tess."

She swallowed hard. "Please, Nick, I can't deal with this right now."

"Hi." Chelsea's voice came like a savior's from the doorway. Dressed simply in blue jeans and an oversize T-shirt, she was pale with a world-weary expression on her face.

For a brief moment, Nick looked annoyed at the interruption, then he quelled his emotion. "Hey there, girl. Come on in. You two can use my office." He rose, circled the desk and laid a hand on Tessa's shoulder. "Promise you won't leave until I get back from my noon meeting."

Why not? She'd broken so many promises, what was one more? She gave Nick her word, which now was about as worthless as monopoly money.

When he left, Chelsea studied her. Sometimes, the young girl had an uncanny ability to sense things about Tessa. "Are you okay, Mrs. L?"

"I'm fine."

"We don't have to do this now."

"No, this works for me. Do you want to get some lunch?"

"Yeah." She placed a hand on her stomach. "The baby needs food."

"Ah."

"You knew, didn't you?"

"I thought maybe."

"I need to talk to somebody about this. A woman. And I admire you so much. You're so together."

How ironic. "I don't know about that, but come on, let's go get something to eat."

Chelsea linked arms with Tessa. As they headed out, Tessa said a prayer to God—who probably wasn't listening to her anymore—that she could do one last worthwhile thing here.

DAN DECIDED it was a sign from fate when he found his brother in Karen's office at lunchtime. He'd been going crazy with all his fears and doubts since the weekend. "Hey, Nick, what are you doing here?" he asked from the open doorway of the assistant D.A.'s office.

"I have a meeting about a couple of my kids who are skirting the law."

"Sorry to hear that."

"Goes with the territory."

"Where's Karen?"

"The mayor dropped by. They stepped out to chat." His brother's grin was broad. "I think it has something to do with your dinner tonight."

Dan leaned against the doorjamb. "Which you're coming to, right?"

Nick didn't answer.

Dan sauntered into the room and leaned against the desk. "Nick, please, I want you there."

"Maybe."

"I've counted you at my table."

"Dan, don't push it. Please."

Dan studied his brother. "Tessa would like it if you were there."

Tessa. Who'd drugged him with sex for forty-eight hours and drew promises out of him he didn't want to keep.

"Something wrong?" Nick asked. "You're scowling."

"Same old, same old."

"Cut her some slack. She'll be fine."

Nick's tone alerted him. "Why do you say that?"

"I just think she will."

"Have you seen her since we got back yesterday?"

"Uh-huh. She was at the center to meet with Chelsea. She's working wonders with those girls."

"Today? She'd told me she had no firm plans. It's one of her days off work and she wanted to do some errands, then get ready for tonight."

"The meeting must have slipped her mind."

Or it was another example of how she was keeping things from him.

"Don't look so annoyed. She'll be ready for tonight."

Dan glanced at his watch. Suddenly, he needed

to see her. "I wonder if she'd want to grab some lunch with me."

"Maybe. If she doesn't eat with Chelsea."

"I'll call her first."

"Sorry, Nick, that was about your brother." Karen came into the office and smiled when she saw Dan. "The man of the hour. Excited about tonight?"

"Oh, yeah, sure."

"Mr. Calm and Cool, always," Nick said. "Even if he has to give a speech to the multitudes."

Dan may have a reputation for unflappability, but right now, he wasn't cool about anything.

His wife had lied to him once again.

FRANKIE WAS LIVID. His head hurt so bad he wanted to punch something. First Trixie had gone away, now she was late getting here today. In his clearer moments, he suspected she hadn't been to a retreat. Her sister didn't know anything about it for one thing. But, just in case, he didn't want to mess with God so he let it go.

Then he'd read in the paper about the Citizen of the Year celebration tonight at the Convention Center. So she wasn't planning to go away with him today. Well, screw this! His duffel bag was all packed. She was leaving town with him today if he had to knock her out and drag her to the car.

But they weren't going anywhere until they had sex. He was through letting her put him off and planned to have her, once again. There was something wrong with her evasion all this time. Especially since she'd called him every day while she was gone and told him she couldn't wait to make love, that she wanted to as soon as she could get to the hotel.

Frankie's hands trembled. All these negative thoughts made him feel funny. He sank onto the mattress, closed his eyes and tried to shake off the confusion and pain brewing in his head.

There was a knock on the door.

He flew off the bed and opened it to find her there, looking beautiful in simple black slacks and a white blouse. Her hair was pulled off her face, though, in some kind of tie. He didn't like it, so before he said anything, he yanked the thing out.

She flinched. "Ouch!"

"Don't wear your hair like that. I hate it."

She eyed him. "What's wrong with you, Frankie?"

Aware of a maid coming down the hall, he dragged her inside. "I'm done." He slammed the door.

"Done with what?"

"You stallin'. Take off your clothes."

Tossing her head back and forth like a wild woman, she reached into her purse. Her hands were shaking bad. "I brought you more money, Frankie."

"I don't want no money. I want you."

"I—"

"Do this now, Trixie, or I'm going to that guy and tell him everything. I've *had* it." He raised his voice on purpose. His father always got his way by yelling. "Do you hear me? I've had it." When he saw fear on her face, he went in for the kill. "Maybe I'll crash that fancy dinner tonight and let everybody in this freakin' town know what's going on. What do you think of that?"

She got so sad. He could take fear. He could take anger. But he hated to see her sad. He *loved* her. Crossing to the dresser, he picked up the roses and brought them to her. "Here, baby, I got you these. Don't be sad."

When tears came to her eyes, he wiped them away. "Shh. They're your favorites. Aren't they?"

Still, she said nothing.

He rubbed his hands up and down the silky blouse she wore. He traced the neckline, and she shuddered with need. "This'll help you stop feeling sad. It always did, doll."

She buried her face in the flowers before he pried them from her hands and tossed them on the bed. Smiling tenderly at her, he undid the first button of her blouse. And the second one.

Then, the door to the room flew open.

The guy who claimed to be her husband loomed in the doorway.

CHAPTER TEN

TESSA SHRIEKED as the door hit the wall and rocked the room. She whirled, clutching her blouse. Dan stood in the doorway. Her first thought was that now this whole charade would be over. He'd finally know the truth about her, and the web of lies she'd lived with for so long would be out in the open. For a brief minute, it brought her an odd sense of peace.

Dan was clearly furious, his hands fisted at his sides. "What's going on here?"

Frankie grabbed Tessa by the arms, making her cry out and sending Dan into action. He leaped across the room and yanked Tessa away from Frankie. She fell into his chest and started to cry. He drew her a few feet back but kept his arm around her, making her feel safe for the first time in days. "Who the *hell* are you?"

"The guy she loves. Frankie Hamilton."

"How do you know Tessa?"

Frankie massaged his temples. "Her name is Trixie."

"What?"

"Trixie Lawrence. You think you're so smart. I was her first boyfriend. The first guy she hit the sheets with. I came to this stupid town to find her and take her away with me."

Dan's bristled in denial. "Are you out of your mind? You must be crazy to make up a story like that."

Grabbing Dan's shirt, Tessa said, "Don't say that—"

But Frankie's booming voice cut her off. "Don't call me crazy. I warn you…"

Tessa cringed in fear. Dan needed to know that Frankie *was* crazy, but he went off when people said he was. She didn't have time to tell her husband, though, before Frankie launched himself across the room.

Dan pushed her away, and she fell to the floor just as Frankie made contact. Dan stumbled backward. He was taller and heavier than Frankie, though Frankie had muscle on him. They went down and Frankie pinned Dan on the rug, his hands around Dan's neck, trying to choke him. Dan maneuvered his arms between Frankie's and, with a surge of strength, broke free. He landed a hard punch in Frankie's face. Bone connected with bone and Frankie fell off him. Reversing their positions, Dan punched him again. Frankie lay on the floor, conscious, but he'd stopped struggling. Tessa grabbed Dan from behind to stop the pummeling.

"Dan, don't. Please, don't."

He held his fist back mid-air.

He looked up at Tessa. Back down at Frankie, whose mouth was bleeding and his face beginning to swell. Dan stood and said nothing. He scanned the room as if he was getting his bearings. Frankie moved on the floor, and Dan put his foot on Frankie's chest. "Stay away from my wife and family."

Like a man coming out of a daze, Dan grabbed Tessa's arm and dragged her out of the room.

The door slammed behind them.

"Dan, I—"

"Shut up."

"What?"

"I said shut up."

He'd never talked to her like that before. Never looked at her with such disgust. He spat out a series of four-letter words she'd never heard him use. Told her to button her blouse.

Tessa no longer felt safe. Or glad Dan had shown up.

She was scared to death.

BECAUSE HE COULDN'T trust himself to speak, Dan was silent on the trip home, though he'd insisted Tessa ride with him and leave her car in the parking lot. His hand throbbed, but his heart was in worse shape. As they drove into the garage, he couldn't even look at his wife. She'd been on the verge of sleeping with another man. He simply couldn't believe it.

Without waiting for her, he got out of the car and stormed into the house. When they reached the kitchen, he threw the keys on the table and faced her. Folding his arms over his chest, he ignored the terror in her face. Just hours ago, it would have sent him to his knees.

"You were going to sleep with that sleazebag."

Expecting a denial, he was shocked when she said, "I don't know what I was going to do."

"Seemed pretty clear to me." He pushed himself away from the counter, strode to the fridge and got a beer. With vicious force, he yanked off the bottle cap and took a long gulp. "How long has this been going on?"

"Frankie came to town about two weeks ago."

Realization slammed into him. "He's the guy I saw in the park."

"Yes."

His hand curled around the bottle. "You let him stalk our little girl and didn't tell me anything about him?"

"I didn't know it was him."

She was lying. His mind was beginning to process the other lies she'd told him. "You promised me at Belhurst Castle that you weren't keeping anything from me."

"I—I didn't know what to do."

"He was at the fair, wasn't he? That's why you were so nervous, why you got sick."

"Yes."

"All those lies, about the deep fryer, about getting your period."

She didn't deny them. She couldn't, of course.

He swore again viciously. "You didn't fall at yoga. He *hit* you."

This time she just nodded. Leaning against the pantry door, she wrapped her hands around her waist. Her face was almost the color of her white blouse. The blouse that guy had his hands on. Was unbuttoning. That inflamed Dan, and he ignored the trembling that had seized his wife.

He slugged back more beer. "So, are you going to explain all this to me?"

"You told me to shut up."

"You can talk now."

"Frankie Hamilton was my first and only boyfriend in Iverton, Ohio, where we grew up. I was plain and shy, and boys didn't pay attention to me. My background was unsavory—you know those details—and not a lot of guys, or girls for that matter, wanted me in their circle of friends."

"He's an ugly old man."

"He's only five years older than me. Prison ages you."

Dan's heartbeat picked up. "He was in prison?"

"Yes. He was sent to Kansas Federal Penitentiary fifteen years ago and got out two weeks ago."

"Did you stay in touch with him?" The notion horrified him.

"No, of course not."

"Why did he come looking for you if you've had no contact?"

"Frankie's obsessed with me. It began the year before he went to prison and got progressively worse. He must have fed on it during his incarceration."

"Why did he come here?"

"He wanted me to leave town with him. I think he has what's called a delusional disorder. At first, when we were young, he was jealous and paranoid. Then the obsession began, and he was unable to see things clearly. I looked it up on the Internet, and the symptoms he has match."

"You've been a busy girl."

"Dan, I'm sorry. I should have told you about him before. But I was afraid."

"With good reason." He shook his head. "There must be more to it than this, though. I thought you loved our life." He swallowed hard. "And me." He hated how his voice broke on the last word.

"I do love you."

Slamming the bottle on the counter, he lurched across the room and grabbed her by the wrists. "Don't you dare say that to me when you were going to sleep with somebody else. Somebody like him." His brain was muddled. "I can't believe it. You were going to throw away our whole life together to sleep with an ex-con who was obsessed with you?"

"Frankie was blackmailing me."

His grip on her tightened. "*What*?"

She tried to pull back, but he kept her wrists in a viselike grip. She flinched.

"Frankie threatened to go to the dinner tonight. To embarrass you by telling everybody about us. I was trying to stop him."

Flinging her away, Dan began to pace. Even with the blackmail part, this still didn't make sense. Then his mind cleared, and he put the pieces together. He rounded on her. "You haven't told me the whole story, have you?"

She drew in a breath. "I was in prison, too."

His head began to buzz. "What did you say?"

"When Frankie went to prison, so did I."

"No, that can't be true."

"It is."

"You're a *criminal*?"

This time, she recoiled as if he had hit her. His first impulse was to haul her to his heart and apologize. Instead, he picked up his beer again. "Tell me the whole story."

Leaning against the counter, as if she needed support, Tessa met his gaze. "When I was nineteen, I was sent to a federal prison camp for eighteen months."

"What did you do?"

"We were in his car. We'd been drinking. Smoking some weed."

"You did marijuana?"

"I did worse than that." Her face had gone blank, and her voice monotone. "We hit another car. Two people died."

"Oh, dear Lord, no."

Tears filled those hazel eyes he loved and coursed down her cheeks. He refused to be moved by them.

"There's got to be more. New York State doesn't consider accidents like that manslaughter unless…"

"Unless you have a traffic violation. Frankie ran the red light."

"Still—fifteen years? And why were you convicted? You weren't driving."

"We were carrying a serious amount of coke in the car. I didn't know it was there or that he was dealing drugs."

Manslaughter? Drugs? "So that's why you were convicted, too."

"Yes."

When it started to sink in and the ramifications became clear, Dan's lawyer's mind tried to assemble the facts. "Let me get this straight. You've lied for years about who you are—a drug addict, promiscuous, it appears, and partly responsible for the death of two people."

She hesistated. "I wasn't an addict." That it was all she could deny made the whole thing worse. "I'm sorry, Dan."

"Sorry? Do you think being *sorry* is enough here?"

"No, of course not." The tears had stopped, but her voice was weak.

He crossed to the trash, tossed his empty beer in the recycle bin and turned to face her. "I don't know what to say." How did you talk when your heart had been smashed into a thousand pieces?

"I was wrong not to tell you about this before. But I was afraid, with your background, you'd hate me."

He didn't deny that. Right now he was feeling a whole barrelful of negative emotions for her.

"You should have at least told me before we got married."

Defiance sparked in her eyes, but she didn't respond.

"Or you could have come clean at any time during our ten years together."

"What would you have done, if I had?"

"I don't know."

"Like I said, I was afraid."

"So, you're a coward in addition to being a slut and a criminal."

For a moment, he felt bad when he saw the expression on her face. Defeat. It was just how she'd looked when he first met her. He began to prowl the kitchen again. He could barely stand the sight of the home she'd made for him.

"I know you feel differently about me now. I expected that. But we have to put it aside. What are we going to do about Frankie? He can ruin everything for us."

"That fact has not escaped me." He shook his head. "I've tried to live a respectable life, and now some two-bit ex-con is going to destroy it." He added, "Because of you."

This time, her tears moved him. He had to stop battering her. "I'm going out for a while."

"All right. What do you want to do about tonight?"

"Tonight?"

"The dinner for your award."

His laugh was ugly.

"You have to go to the ceremony."

"Maybe."

"I can say I'm sick. I don't have to be there, if you'd rather I wasn't."

"No." Why was he saying this? The last thing he wanted was to spend time with a woman he didn't even know. "You'll go as planned. The kids are with Brad's parents. Everybody's coming. We'll do this one last thing together."

"And then?"

"What do you mean?"

"C-can you ever forgive me?"

"It isn't a matter of forgiveness." Was it? "It's a matter of trust."

"I can earn back your trust."

An image of the guy's hands on her blouse raged through him. "What about your boyfriend? When he makes your sordid background known, do you honestly think we can go on from there?"

Her body sagged and she gripped the countertop.
"I guess not."

"We're getting ahead of ourselves. You've got to
go to the dinner. Act as if nothing happened."

"I'm not sure I can do that."

"Why not?" He stared at her. "You've been acting
like a pro for ten years. One more night shouldn't
make any difference, *Trixie*."

Her eyes were so bleak he had to look away.
Brushing past her to the door, he ignored the sound
of her weeping that followed him out.

"HERE, DRINK THIS. You'll feel better."

Tessa stared at the steaming tea Janey set in front
of her and wanted to die. "Nothing will ever make
me feel better again." She closed her eyes. "You
should have seen him, Janey. What he said was bad
enough, but he looked at me with such revulsion."
She buried her face in her hands. What Dan had said,
his disgust, would haunt her forever. He was right.
For the first time, she realized you couldn't really
overcome your past.

Janey tilted her chin and took up the role again of
the older sister who could make everything all right.
If only Tessa had listened to her when she was
young. "Dan's in shock. He doesn't know what he's
saying or doing. This is a knee-jerk reaction."

"Problem with knee-jerk reactions is they show a
person's real feelings."

"Not necessarily. His need for respectability because of his father is what caused his reaction. I think he'll come around."

Tessa knew in her heart that wasn't true. She was also angry at Dan for turning on her. Deep down she must have believed her husband would stand by her unconditionally.

"It's that bastard's fault," Janey said. "If he hadn't come to town, this wouldn't have happened."

"He's sick, Janey. He thinks I wrote him letters. He thinks I called him to say I wanted to have sex with him."

"Oh, honey. I'm so sorry." Janey dropped into a chair. "All right. Let's plan. I have some money. Maybe we can bribe him to keep quiet."

"I tried that. It didn't work."

"We could try again."

"Thanks, Janey, but no. I have to handle this myself."

"No way. I'll stop him from ruining your life if it's the last thing I do. I'm not abandoning you in this."

Like Dan had.

Tessa's cell phone rang. *Please, God, let it be Dan.* Contacting her would indicate some kind of concern. "Hello."

"Mrs. Logan? It's Chelsea Chamberlain." The girl's voice was strained, panicky.

Tessa swallowed back her own anxiety. "Hi, Chelsea."

"You said I could call you anytime."

She bit her lip. "What do you need, sweetie?"

"Something's wrong. Really wrong. Please come."

"Where are you?"

"In the park, by your house. I came over here…" She started to cry, and a huge moan escaped her, as if she was in pain.

"I'll be right there, Chels. Sit tight." Clicking off, Tessa stood, grateful that she'd had Janey drive her to the hotel where Frankie was staying to pick up her car.

"What?"

"It's one of Nick's kids. She's in trouble."

"Tessa, *you're* in trouble. You can't go running off to help some kid you barely know."

"She reminds me of who I used to be, Janey. If I can help her, I'm going to. Besides, I can't do anything for myself, but maybe I can for Chelsea."

Janey glanced at the clock. "The girls?"

"Are being picked up by Brad's mother because of the dinner tonight. You know all this." She stopped when she got to the door and glanced back. "Your support and trust mean more to me than I can say."

Neither of which Dan had given her.

LIKE A MADMAN, Dan had driven to Nick's place of work because he didn't know where else to go. When he'd got to the center, his brother took one look at him, shut his office door and sat behind his desk. Dan leaned against the wall and, choking on the words, spilled out the whole sordid story.

Thoughtful, Nick steepled his hands. "That poor woman."

"What?"

"I said, poor Tessa. It's hell trying to live with that kind of secret."

Again Dan cursed.

Angling his head, Nick sighed. "Dan, look, I know you're upset. But is respectability more important than your wife?"

"My wife is not the person I thought she was."

"Of course she is. Look what she's made of herself after a bad childhood. After a tragic mistake she's had to live with for the rest of her life."

"None of that makes any difference to me."

Nick appeared startled. "I see."

Pushing off from the wall, Dan dropped into the chair in front of Nick's desk. "What I said doesn't apply to you."

"Of course it does. I hadn't realized you felt that way about things being irrevocable, about not being able to make up for past actions."

"I don't. I'm proud of what you've done with your life."

"If I buy that, then you should be proud of Tessa."

"You're kidding, right? She broke the law. She went to jail. And then she lied to me all these years."

"Because you're such a nut about your reputation,

about being respectable. She was probably scared to death."

"Goddamn it, she was going to sleep with the guy to keep him quiet."

Again, his brother was thoughtful. "Did she say she was going to do that?"

"She said she didn't know what she was going to do."

"She wouldn't have slept with him."

"He had his hands on her blouse! It was unbuttoned!"

"She wouldn't have done it."

"How do you know?"

"She's a loving wife who doesn't even know other men exist. She'd never hook up with another guy. Hell, she didn't even want to work with my boys."

"You don't think straight when it comes to Tessa, Nick. I suspect you're a little bit in love with her."

"*Everybody's* a little bit in love with her."

Dan hit the desk with his open hand. It still hurt from punching out that bastard, as did the bruises on his neck. "Including Frankie Hamilton. My God, he calls her *Trixie*."

Standing, Nick came around the desk and leaned on it. "Dan, don't do anything stupid. Let this settle. Try to be understanding."

"Of *what?*"

"You don't get it do you?"

"Get what?"

"Tessa was trying to protect you. Even if she was going to sleep with this guy, which I don't think is the case, she was doing it for you."

Dan closed his eyes to block out the images of her with anyone else.

"You need to deal with what this guy's going to do now."

"I know. Tessa said he threatened to go to the dinner tonight if she didn't…" He couldn't finish the blasphemous sentence.

"I'll come to the dinner. In case anything happens."

"Even though Mom will be there?"

"Yes."

Dan stood. "All right." He glanced at his watch. "I'm going to take a drive. Clear my head. Then go home and get ready."

"Want me to go with you?"

"No, I need to be alone."

"All right."

Dan squeezed his brother's shoulder and headed for the door.

"Dan?"

He turned back.

"If she was my wife, I'd do anything to protect her from all this."

The thought shamed Dan. *He'd* attacked his wife. Berated her. How was she going to handle that on top of everything else?

Damn it, he wasn't going to feel sorry for her. Worry about her. She'd lied to him all these years about who she was and what she'd done. And he'd never forget that.

FRANKIE OPENED HIS EYES to look at the red numbers of the digital clock—4:00 p.m. It was light outside, though the room was dim. He sank back onto the bed. He had time yet to get ready for tonight's dinner, so he'd only stay here a minute. Pain still battered his eyelids and his temples. And his hands ached. The guy had done a number on him. And Trixie hadn't stopped him. She'd helped him. How could she do that?

Burying his face into the pillow, he took comfort in the fact that she'd called him a few minutes ago. Told him to put on his nice blue suit and meet her at the Citizen of the Year dinner. They'd go public about what was what, then they'd leave town together.

His back was to the door when he heard it whisper open. The freakin' jerk had broken the lock. Must be Trixie, coming back to see him. Rolling over, he saw a figure silhouetted in the light from the corridor.

"Hello, Frankie."

CHAPTER ELEVEN

CHECKING HIS WATCH, Dan drew in a breath and tried not to let his pique show to the crowd milling around him at the Convention Center. And he refused to worry about Tessa. It was seven o'clock and she still wasn't there. He hadn't seen her since he'd left the house at about three. After he'd gone to talk to Nick, Dan had driven around for a long time. Despite his brother's advice, he didn't know how he and Tessa could work this out. Still, he admitted some things to himself, some things he was ashamed of. He'd spoken cruelly to her and touched her roughly, something he'd never done before. In his mind, he saw again her horror at his initial reaction. And her disappointment. He'd attacked her. Chagrined, he'd finally driven home to talk to her.

And she wasn't there. His first thought was she'd gone to see the asshole again. He'd thrown a vase across the room, all recriminations for his earlier behavior forgotten. At six, he'd taken a shower, dressed, and still she hadn't shown up. He'd left the house, more concerned about her welfare than he wanted to be. But she was an experienced woman, not the innocent naive girl he'd fallen in love with. She could take care of herself.

"Dan?" the mayor said behind him. Dressed meticulously, like Dan, Mitch Nash was grinning. "Ready for the big event?"

I've already had it. "Yes. I am. Thank you again for nominating me."

"It was unanimous among the council members." He clapped Dan on the back. "Where's that beautiful wife of yours?"

"She's meeting me here. I'm afraid she's a bit late."

Mitch glanced over Dan's shoulder. "Ah, now there's a sight."

"Tessa?" He whirled around.

"No, your mother." She was coming toward them, elegant and cool in a trim, pearl-gray suit. "Hello, dear." She kissed Dan's cheek, then raised her gaze to the mayor. "Mitchell."

"You're looking beautiful as ever, Claire."

They made chitchat while Dan kept an eye on the door. Tessa didn't come through it.

But Janey did. For the first time since he'd known Tessa's sister, she wasn't put together. Her dress was fine, but her shoes didn't match it and her hair was mussed.

Claire stood aside so she could join them. "Hello, Janey."

"Mayor. Claire." Even Janey's voice was raw. "Congratulations," she said coldly to Dan.

"Thanks."

Janey frowned. "Where's Tessa? She said she was coming when I saw her this afternoon."

So that was why Janey was disheveled. Tessa had told her the whole story. Unless she knew it all along. That notion incensed Dan. He'd just get calmed down and something new would happen, like Tessa not coming home or the possibility that she'd trusted her sister with this and not him, and he'd lose perspective.

"Of course she's coming," he snapped.

"Why on earth wouldn't she?" the mayor asked.

Janey was scowling now. "No reason."

"Won't Brad be here, dear?" Dan's mother asked.

"No, he couldn't get back from London." She shrugged. "I'm supposed to go over there on the 6:00 a.m. flight tomorrow to meet him."

"I'm sorry he isn't here for Dan's big night."

"Me, too. We need him now."

Claire cocked her head—at the odd remark?—but before she could say more, the mayor touched her arm. "Claire, come with me. I want to introduce you to my son."

The older couple excused themselves and walked away.

Dan faced Janey head-on. "Where the hell is she?"

"What do you care, you son of a bitch?"

Her fury startled him. But then, why was he surprised? Janey was like a lionness with her cub around Tessa. She'd do anything for her. Even lie for her all these years. "Did you know he'd come back?"

"None of your business."

"That's what I thought. Seems I'm the only one who was in the dark."

Janey straightened her shoulders in a gesture Tessa affected when she went on the defensive. "You know, I thought you were the answer to her prayers. Instead, you've become her worst nightmare."

"Janey, I'm the injured party here."

"You're kidding, right? Do you have any idea how *wounded* Tessa is? She was able to recover somewhat after what happened to her when she was young because of you and the life you built together. But in a few short hours, you've destroyed all that."

"I didn't destroy anything. She did. By her lies and cover-ups."

Janey continued as if he hadn't spoken. "She was so despondent, so hopeless when she came over to my house this afternoon. Just like she was when she got out of prison. She's never going to get over your reaction to this. From what you said to her. I'm really worried about her."

What the hell was wrong with this woman? There was no defense for what Tessa had done. "She didn't come home all day. Do you know where she is now?"

Janey's eyes teared up. "I don't know. I've been

trying her cell and she won't answer." She took a bead on him. "Oh, Lord, don't tell me. She's been missing all this time, and you didn't even try to call her?"

How on earth could he feel like the guilty party?

He didn't have time to ask Janey that because his brother came up behind her. He looked like hell, too. His cheeks were pale and his eyes weary. He held himself stiffly.

"Dan." He kissed Janey's cheek. "Janey. Where's Tessa?"

"She's not here."

"Isn't she coming?"

"We don't know."

Another fulminating look from her sister. "Serves you right if she doesn't."

"I'll say she's sick."

"A lie?" Janey mocked him. "Why, Dan, you wouldn't."

He was about to defend himself when Tessa appeared in the doorway. To the casual observer, she didn't look as if anything was wrong. She was stunning in a white sheath, which dipped enough in the front to be sophisticated but modest. But Dan could see the telltale signs of strain, the despair in her eyes, her tight mouth and the stiffness of her shoulders. Janey was right, she'd only looked like this once before, when he'd first met her.

Making her way across the room, Tessa gave Nick

and Janey each a peck on the cheek and said hello to them. She turned to Dan. "Hi." No kiss. No touch. He noticed she wasn't wearing her pearls. Was that some kind of signal to him?

"Where have you been?" he asked.

Instead of answering, she addressed Nick. "I tried to call you on your cell phone. You didn't answer."

His brother fidgeted. "I, um, had to go out. What is it?"

"It's about one of your girls from the center. I need to speak with you in private," she said, leading him away.

"What the hell?" Dan said.

"Get used to it. If I were her, I'd never trust you again."

Tessa not trust *him!* Everybody's reaction to this was upside down.

But he had no time to deal with Janey as Patricia Clemens, the mayor's assistant, who'd organized the celebratory dinner, approached. "Dan, you and your family need to sit. We'd like to begin."

Some celebration, he thought.

TESSA TRIED TO INURE herself to the sight of Dan at the podium, accepting his award. Since she had left Janey's, she'd kept her emotions on a tight leash. She had to steer clear of the self-pity that threatened to engulf her, so she'd focused her attention on helping Chelsea. But now, coming face-to-face with what she'd done, and what she'd never have back in her life because of it, challenged her control. So she blocked out Dan and turned her thoughts to the young girl.

The seventeen-year-old had had a miscarriage, like Tessa had with their first child. Chelsea was bleeding when Tessa met her at the park, and they'd raced to the hospital. Not knowing whom to call or what to do, Tessa had tried to reach Nick, but he hadn't answered his cell. She'd sat with the girl the entire time. After dinner, Chelsea took the decision of who to alert away from Tessa by calling her parents. After they'd arrived, Tessa had had just enough time to go home, change and get to the Convention Center.

"I hope I've done justice to the district attorney position." Dan smiled at the audience with his trademark charisma. It broke her heart that he'd never smile at her again. To avoid looking at him, she studied the crowd.

She'd felt some relief when she'd arrived at the Convention Center and discovered attendees needed a ticket to get in. That meant Frankie wouldn't be allowed through the door. He could hang around outside, maybe accost them in the parking garage, but she refused to think about that. She'd deal with whatever she had to when it happened.

"I believe in punishment for crimes. Even for youthful offenders."

No surprise there.

"But I also believe in rehabilitation. In making our

world one where we can all…" here he stumbled over his words "…have a second chance."

She glanced at Janey, who was glaring at Dan. Nick touched Tessa's arm. He knew. Dan had gone there to talk to him.

What did it matter who knew? Soon, Dan would cut her out of his life and everyone would find out about her failed marriage. *If* Frankie didn't show up tonight and reveal everything before Dan made the decision.

Her husband received a standing ovation. Patty Clemens touched her shoulder from behind. "Tessa, the press would like a picture of you and Dan."

Conspicuously absent from his speech had been any thanks to his wife and family. And he hadn't called her up front to join him at the end, as he'd planned to do.

Rising, Tessa made her way to the podium with as much grace as she could muster.

She didn't break down when she kissed him on the cheek and he went still.

She didn't shrink from him when he stiffened as she slid her arm around his waist.

Instead, she smiled for the camera.

So did Dan.

Apparently, she wasn't the only good actor in the family.

TOO FAST, DAN PULLED into his garage and was stupidly relieved to see Tessa's car in its place.

They'd stayed to talk to reporters, and when the festivities were over he was surprised to find Janey and Nick had waited for them outside the ballroom. His mother had gotten a ride with Mayor Nash.

"Come home with me, Tessa," Janey had said as they'd all headed to the parking garage. "You're taking me to the airport at dawn anyway. Stay the night."

Tessa had hesitated. Dan could tell she was tempted by the offer.

He jumped in. "She's going back to our house."

"I'm not sure that's a good idea," Nick said.

"I don't give a shit what either of you say. We're going home together."

"Why?" Janey asked. "So you can torture her more?"

"Janey. Please." Tessa's resignation tore at him. "Don't make this worse."

"Could it be any worse?"

They all knew it could be. What Frankie Hamilton would do was still unknown.

"Listen, I'm going to stop at the hospital to see one of my kids," Nick said. "Then I can come over to your house. Maybe I can help you two talk this out." He tried to joke. "I have counseling degrees, you know."

"No, Nick." Tessa's voice had been monotone and clearly without hope. "I'll be fine. Give Chelsea my best. Tell her I'll call her tomorrow."

Dan hadn't understood the exchange, but he'd

been too mired in his own misery to ask about it. The valet had delivered Tessa's car first, and she'd left without speaking to him. As a matter of fact, she'd said almost nothing to him all night. Could she possibly be angry with him? Janey certainly was. Funny, he'd been glad about Janey's protectiveness before. He'd *thought* Tessa needed a protector. Little did he know she'd taken care of herself for two years in prison.

For the first time it hit him that she might have endured unspeakable things there. He felt sick to his stomach.

He came in through the kitchen and caught sight of her by the window in the family room, still dressed in her evening clothes. He grabbed himself some wine and was about to ask her if she wanted some. Old habits died hard, he guessed. He made his way to the adjacent room with one glass in his hand.

Staring out, she watched the rain patter against the glass. Fitting that it had started to downpour.

"Where'd you go?" he asked.

When she turned at the sound of his voice, her expression revealed nothing. "Go?"

"Before the dinner?"

"Does it matter?"

He sank onto the couch. His body ached with exhaustion, but he was all coiled up, ready to strike. "Did you go see him? Pay up, so to speak, so he didn't come to the dinner tonight?" Dan hadn't realized that was what he was thinking until he spoke the words out loud. And how incensed the notion made him.

She just stared at him with wide, hollow eyes.

"Our torrid night of sex at the Belhurst Castle?"

"What about it?"

He shook his head. "I should have suspected something then. You…did things…knew things about making love that we never experienced together."

Her jaw tightened, and her face lost its meager color. "Just to set the record straight, at Belhurst Castle I was desperate and wanted to make love to you as intimately as I could. Nothing I did was planned or calculated." Her lips trembled. "And I acted out of instinct. Not from something I learned with anyone else."

"You expect me to believe that?"

Shaking her head, she stared at him. "This is how it's going to be, isn't it?"

"How what's going to be?"

"How you're going to treat me."

"What did you expect, Tessa? That I'd say, 'Oh, honey, I'm so sorry about your past, but don't worry this can be fixed. I'll stand by you no matter what'?"

Her eyes filled. "That's what I would have done for you."

The impact of her statement was like a hard blow to his chest. "Damn it, Tessa. I won't let you make me feel guilty. You're the one who's ruined our lives."

A tear coursed down her cheek. "I know."

"Maybe if you'd told me in the beginning…"

"I did my best to stay away from you, Dan."

He hadn't forgotten. The memories came back to him…

No, Dan, I won't go out with you. We're so mismatched.

Dan, please, don't pursue this with me. You're almost engaged. She's the kind of woman you deserve.

Of course I've come to care about you. You've given me no choice in the matter. I'll sleep with you but I won't get serious.

No, Dan, don't look so happy. My being pregnant is a tragedy. I can't marry a man like you. I just can't.

"I haven't forgotten your resistance," he admitted. "But damn it, Tessa, you knew how I felt about lies…respectability."

She swallowed hard. "You're right. I should have been stronger. I should have told you then about my past, and you would have left me alone. At the very least, I should have said no to your advances." She touched her stomach. "When I found out I was having your child, I felt vulnerable, and I loved you so much. Still, I shouldn't have given in."

In truth, there was no way in hell he would have let her go when she was pregnant. He didn't share that thought with her, though.

"What are we going to do now?" Her voice was a whisper. "I know it will never be the same between us."

"That's about the only thing I'm sure of."

"Well, there are two things I'm sure of."

"What?"

She was like David facing down Goliath. "I want another chance. I want to rebuild our marriage. Even if it can't be the same, I'd like to try to make it something different. Maybe even something better."

"I don't think I can do that."

Her chest heaved. "All right. Then the second thing I'm sure of is this. I'll never give up my children. You can cut me out of your life, but not theirs."

His kids. Innocent Sara. Mischievous Molly. It hit him now, where his older child had got her wild streak. "Not even if you're a bad influence on them? Especially Molly."

She wavered and used the wall to steady herself. She didn't speak for a minute. And Dan realized he'd never said anything more cruel to anyone in his life. He wanted to take it back. "Tess, I—"

Her hand went up, palm out. "No, don't say any more. I'm not sure I can stand it." She drew in a breath. And another. "I'll go to Janey's tonight. Brad's mother is taking the kids to school tomorrow, so I won't be missed in the morning."

"You're not driving like this."

She cocked her head. "I'll be taking care of myself from now on, Dan. And my children, regardless of what you think." She wiped away

another tear. "I'm sorry I've done this to our lives."
She escaped to the kitchen.

"Tessa, wait."

But she didn't. The door to the garage closed, and
he heard the bay door go up. In minutes, she was gone.

TESSA DIDN'T SLEEP all night. She lay in Janey's guest
room, tossing and turning, trying to come to terms
with what had happened, worrying about Sara and
Molly. And Dan.

She cried off and on for her daughters and what
this would do to them. For the death of a life that had
been so perfect she should have known it couldn't
last. For women like her, anyway. Secrets always
came out. Inner flaws were always revealed. You
couldn't really change who you were. At four, she
heard Janey stir so she got out of bed.

Tessa went downstairs ready to go to the airport
and found Janey in the kitchen making coffee. Her
sister was even more haggard than last night, edgy
and unnerved. She wasn't even dressed yet.

"You didn't sleep."

"No." Janey brushed back her hair. "You?"

"No." She touched her sister's arm. "I'm sorry
you're so tired when you have an international flight
to take today."

"Tessa, I don't think I should go."

"I won't hear of it, Janey. You can't miss Brad's
kickoff dinner or the festivities the day before."

"You need me."

"I'll need you when you get back, too. Now go get dressed and bring down your suitcase."

"Are you sure, honey?"

"Of course." She glanced at her watch. "We have to hurry to make the plane."

After dropping Janey off at the airport, Tessa returned to Janey's and not her own house. She couldn't face Dan. While she sipped her coffee at the table, she flipped on the TV to distract her from her awful thoughts.

The Channel 13 anchor was talking and super-imposed over the woman's face was a picture—of Tessa and Dan, smiling like a happy couple. The anchor said something about the dinner last night, and their relationship, then the picture disappeared. Thank God. Tessa's heart could stand only so many blows.

"In other news—" the anchor continued "—the bizarre death of Franklin Hamilton stymies police. He was found in a hotel room in downtown Orchard Place, allegedly struck by a blunt instrument. Police believe a table lamp found at the scene is the murder weapon. The victim bled to death, even though an anonymous caller dialed 911 from the hotel's hall phone to say a man had been hurt. Police believe the caller may have been involved in the death. An investigation into who Hamilton is and why he was in Orchard Place is under way. Authorities believe that link will lead them to determine if this is a homicide and, if so, why Hamilton was killed."

Tessa's mug hit the table and tipped over. Coffee splattered everywhere, onto the oak surface, onto Janey's peach sweat suit, which Tessa had borrowed.

Frankie was dead? Frankie was *dead?* Oh, dear God, the poor man. He was sick and delusional, but he didn't deserve this. Who could have killed him? Forcing herself to be calm, Tessa cleaned up the mess, left Janey's house, locked up and drove down the deserted street to her own home. It was all over the radio stations about the alleged homicide in downtown Orchard Place.

Ten minutes after hearing the broadcast, Tessa walked into her house. Dan was at the kitchen table, staring down at something. As she got closer, she saw he was reading the morning paper. He lifted his head and stared at her. Finally he asked, "Did you kill him?"

Tessa's stomach churned. With those four simple words, her and Dan's relationship was over.

CHAPTER TWELVE

THE WORDS CAME OUT of Dan's mouth before he realized what he'd said. Tessa grabbed the counter. At first, she said nothing but stared at him as if he'd shot her through the heart. In a way, he had.

"No." When she spoke, her tone was once again emotionless. "Of course I didn't kill him."

"You were missing all afternoon."

"I wasn't missing. I was with one of Nick's kids."

So, she had an alibi. Thank God. Somewhere in the back of Dan's mind, he was relieved that she wouldn't be arrested. All night long, he'd rerun the past few weeks in his mind and the number of times she'd blatantly told him an untruth. Not to mention all the lies of omission through the years and hedging about her past. But at least she wouldn't be accused of this crime.

For several moments, she stood there, silent, desolate. Finally, she cleared her throat. "You don't believe me. You think I'm capable of something like this. But you can check it out."

"Since you're so good at lying, maybe I should."

No response.

"Aren't you going to ask me if I did it?"

"No."

"Why?"

Crossing to the sink, she poured herself some water. She gulped it down, and set the glass in the basin. Her movements were stiff, robotic. "I don't need to ask you. I know that under no circumstances could you have killed someone." She watched him as if he was a stranger. "And you should know the same thing about me."

Dan felt small. And stupid. He didn't like the emotions but curbed the urge to strike out again.

"What are we going to do about Frankie's death, Dan?"

"Go to the police. I'll call Lieutenant Dickens right now. He's in charge of homicide." Dan stood. "We have to tell him our relationship to Hamilton, if he hasn't already discovered it. The cops will be on top of an unexplained murder in downtown Orchard Place, even if the guy was some scumbag ex-con."

A tiny gasp escaped her.

"What, do you feel bad that your boyfriend's dead?"

"Of course I do. He was a human being, not some nameless body you can label with insulting epithets. He had a terrible life, and there was something mentally wrong with him. Don't you feel bad he's dead?"

Did he feel bad, after what the guy had done to Tessa?

When Dan didn't answer, she gave him a pitying look. "Despite who he was, I can't figure out who could have killed him. Here in Orchard Place."

"Any number of people. With his past, there could be a lot of shady characters gunning for him." He remembered something. "Did the people you killed leave behind any family?"

Tessa flinched. "A father. He was quoted in the newspaper on the day of Frankie's release saying that somebody like him should die behind bars. Worse yet, be executed."

More information he didn't want, more information that spiked his anger. "You kept tabs on Frankie?"

"No, I wanted to forget he existed."

"Then how do you know about the father's comments when the guy was released?"

"Janey read the *Iverton Banner* online most days. She printed off that article when Frankie got out of prison."

"You and Janey have a lot of secrets. She knew all along, didn't she? She was in collusion with you to hide your past all along."

"Stop it! A man was murdered. It's a terrible thing. And we're in the middle of it. Call Dickens. We need to move on this."

He wasn't thinking clearly. They couldn't afford to wallow in their personal circumstances. He rose and crossed to the phone.

Within a half hour, Mark Dickens arrived with his

assistant, Nell Cumberland. About Dan's age, the police lieutenant was a short, wiry man, with a shrewd look in his eyes. Dan had worked with him on many occasions and knew him to be a bloodhound. Cumberland was shrewd in her own right and always asked pointed questions during an interview. Which was why Dan should have expected it when Dickens said, "I was about to call you."

Tessa nodded to the left. "Let's go into the living room." When they were seated, Dan started to speak, but Tessa held up her hand. "No, I brought Frankie here. I'll talk."

"Tessa, don't say anything you'll regret later."

"They'll find out anyway." She focused on Dickens. "Lieutenant, Frankie Hamilton and I knew each other years ago."

Dickens glanced down at his notes. "In Iverton, Ohio. We finished a background check on him this morning, which of course revealed his connection with you." The officer's gaze intensified. "You were with him in the traffic accident that resulted in the death of two people. You were both sent to jail. Want to give me your version of all that?"

As she did, the only time she cried was when she talked about the woman and child who were killed. The fact that she tried to stifle her tears made watching her harder. Dan resisted the urge to join her on the couch and hold her hand. She clamped her fingers together in her lap through the entire recitation.

"We know the husband—Ike Summers—is still living in Iverton."

"Yes." She filled him in about Janey going online and the comments Summers had made to the press. Dan recognized that the surviving family member could be a suspect.

"How did Hamilton find you?"

"I have no idea."

Cumberland fired off the next question. "Did you write him letters in prison?"

"No."

The cops were on a fishing expedition. He started to tell Tessa not to say anymore, when the lieutenant added, "We found stacks of letters from you in his possession."

Dumbstruck, Dan's jaw dropped. Just minutes ago she'd told him she'd had no contact with Hamilton in prison. Was she still lying to him?

Tessa shook her head. "I'm sure you're well aware, Lieutenant, that the letters in his possession were not written by me."

"Who do you think wrote them?"

"He wrote them himself. That would be easy to verify."

"Why in hell would he do something like that?" Dan asked.

Tessa addressed her explanation to the cops. "I think Frankie had what's called a delusional disorder." She described his behavior years ago and what she'd matched it with on the Internet.

"And in the present?" the lieutenant wanted to know.

"He thought I wrote to him. He thought I called him. He thought I was leaving town with him."

Dickens glanced at Dan, then back to her. "And you weren't?"

"No, Lieutenant. I loved my life here. The kids—" Her voice cracked. She was a good enough mother to be worried about the effect of this on all of them. "I just tried to go on after what happened to me when I was nineteen."

"Until Hamilton came to town and threatened to ruin it."

"Yes. I guess you just can't put the past behind you."

"Did your husband know Hamilton showed up in Orchard Place?"

"No, not until yesterday afternoon."

"Did you know her background, Dan?"

Dan shook his head.

"What did you do when you found out? That Hamilton was here in town?"

Knowing they'd discover this anyway, Dan related the events of the afternoon, including how he'd fought with Hamilton. Dan's DNA would be under Hamilton's fingernails, his prints all over the hotel room.

Cumberland wrote everything in her notebook.

Dickens asked, "Can you tell me your whereabouts yesterday afternoon from about three to seven, Mrs. Logan?"

By rote, Tessa told him she was with Chelsea all afternoon, about the roommate the girl had had in the E.R. and the nurses and doctors who could verify Tessa's whereabouts. Again, Cumberland took down the information, asking for clarification and names.

Without reacting, Dan listened to the details of her alibi.

"And you?" Dickens asked Dan. "Where were you during that time?"

Dan's mind went blank. *Oh, my God.* "I was upset after we came home from the hotel. I went to see my brother, then drove around until I had to get ready for the dinner."

"What time was that?"

"I left here about three. I left Nick's around four."

It was obvious to everyone in the room that Dan had no alibi during the time of the murder.

The lieutenant and his assistant stood. "I think it would be best if you both came to the station house with us. I'd like to talk to you further and check out Mrs. Logan's alibi."

Tessa clasped her elbows with her hands. "Are we being arrested?"

"No. This is a voluntary request."

"What does that mean, Dan?"

"It means they aren't taking either of us into custody." Yet. "This is voluntary accompaniment, no restraints, no locked doors. We'll be free to go any time."

"Should we call a lawyer?"

Dan stood. "No. They already know what's happened or will find out in even a cursory investigation, anyway. Our cooperation will go a long way in proving our innocence, if this gets that far."

Neither Dan nor Tessa spoke much on the trip to the precinct. They were brought to an interview room with windows and soft-blue walls. The police provided coffee for them and told them they were free to use the bathroom, their cell phones.

It soon became clear that the cops were way ahead of them. Several incriminating facts had been discovered. When Dan told them about following Tessa to the hotel room, they already had a witness who saw someone matching Dan's description at the scene. They had indeed gathered DNA from under Frankie's fingernails and off his face, which was currently being examined in a rush job at the lab. They knew Tessa had visited the hotel several times. Not only had she been seen going in and out, but her fingerprints were all over the room. Those were on file from her prison days and had come up as a match in the computer.

After an hour, the detectives left Tessa and Dan alone. When they returned, they told Tessa she was free to go. Chelsea Chamberlain and doctors and nurses had confirmed her whereabouts.

"What about Dan?"

"We'd like you to stay, Dan. We have some more questions for you."

Dan watched them.

"We want DNA from you—" Dickens nodded to Dan's bruised knuckles and bruises on his neck "—which you shouldn't mind giving since you've admitted to the brawl and want to be cooperative."

"I'm not going any further without a lawyer," Dan said.

Dickens nodded. "I figured that."

"Oh, my Lord, no." Tessa gripped Dan's arm. "My husband could never have done this. Never. Please, it's all my fault. You should be blaming me."

Dickens's expression was sympathetic. "I'm sorry, Mrs. Logan. Your alibi checks out. Your husband has none. We have to question him further."

"He could *never* have done this." Her tone was panic-stricken.

Dan swallowed hard at her defense.

"For what it's worth, knowing you, Dan, I can't believe it, either. But I'm proceeding on the facts. You can call your lawyer now."

"Am I in custody?"

"No. You're still here voluntarily."

Tessa began to cry. "Don't stay, Dan."

"I will, but with a lawyer. Go on home, Tessa."

"What?"

"I said go home."

"I'm not leaving. I'm staying with you."

"I'm afraid that isn't possible, Mrs. Logan. We'll need to interrogate your husband alone. You have to exit the area."

"I'll wait outside."

Dan's patience thinned. "The kids have a half day of school, today. You have to go home."

"I know that. But…" She shrugged. "I should be here with you, too."

His frustration reaching its peak, he snapped, "I don't want you here, Tessa."

"Please don't say that. Please."

Dan shook his head. "There's nothing else to say. Go home to the girls."

TESSA HAD NO CHOICE but to leave Dan at the precinct. He didn't want her there, and she had to be home when the girls got there. She wouldn't tell them anything yet, not until she found out if Dan was going to be arrested. But before she got in her car, she called Nick on his cell and asked him to meet her at their house.

Her brother-in-law arrived just as she did. He took one look at her, put his arm around her and accompanied her inside. They made their way to the patio and sat under an umbrella table in the backyard, in sunshine far too bright for what was happening in her life.

"What's going on, Tess?"

She filled him in on Frankie's death.

"Oh, honey. I saw it on the news, but I didn't make the connection. The police weren't releasing any details about it, and Dan never told me Hamilton's name."

He drew her close. Tessa let herself be held. She'd wanted Dan to touch her so much, to give her physical comfort, to indicate he might have some feelings left for her. But, of course, he didn't and would probably never hold her again. So she took solace from Nick's embrace. "You can cry, you know."

"No, I can't. I can't break down. The girls will be home any minute, and I can't let them know anything is wrong."

"I can take them out for a while."

Drawing back, she peered up into a face so full of understanding it almost did her in. Would Dan ever look at her like that again?

"Maybe that would be for the best. I'd like to be alone with Dan as soon as he comes home."

"How is he?"

"Overwrought."

"And taking it out on you."

"That doesn't matter."

Nick let loose with a few expletives.

"Don't, Nick. He needs your support."

The girls were bursting with energy when they rumbled into the house. School was ending soon, and they were always fever-pitched at this time of year.

"We've got a picnic tomorrow." Molly announced.

"I know, sweetie. I'm making cookies for it."

"Uncle Nick, wanna play ball in the park?" Sara asked.

"I think that might make my day." He stood. "Get a jacket, too, because afterward I'm taking you to the lakefront to eat and maybe find an ice-cream stand."

Excited squeals and girlish giggles followed them out.

But Tessa got a queasy feeling in her stomach watching them. The arrest of a district attorney would be a county-wide scandal. Dan's worst nightmare. And it would harm their children.

Nick called her over the next few hours, but she still hadn't heard from Dan. As the day wore on, she made the kids cookies for tomorrow, and with each passing hour she became more and more despairing. Nick brought the girls back after supper; they had showers and climbed into bed. Dan's silence, the absence of communication, was punishment, she guessed, for what she'd done to him. She deserved it. All of it—his loathing, his anger, his contempt.

Still, she wasn't prepared for when he walked into the house at ten o'clock. With Allison Markham.

FATIGUE SETTLED OVER DAN like a shroud as he entered the kitchen. He'd been unable to sleep the night before, had endured a hellish day and could barely put one foot in front of the other. And he had yet to deal with Tessa. He was foggy about what he'd said to her when she'd got home from Janey's that morning. But he knew it wasn't good. And he'd treated her harshly at the station house, too.

She was standing in the kitchen. Dressed in a simple pink shirt and capris, she looked young and innocent. Without any trace of rancor, she asked, "Are you all right?"

He shook his head. "I made it through the day." Crossing to the fridge, he took out two beers and handed one to Allison.

Accepting the drink, Allison said, "Hello, Tessa."

Tessa greeted Allison, then asked Dan, "What happened? Did they arrest you?"

"No." Dan's voice was weary. "But we think they will."

"Tell me why."

He snorted. "Oh, maybe because I was seen kicking in the door of Hamilton's hotel room. Maybe because I beat the crap out of a guy who was blackmailing my wife and threatening my entire life right before he was murdered. Evidence is stacked against me. I had motive, opportunity and can be placed at the scene of the crime. I've prosecuted cases with less circumstantial evidence."

"All because of me. I'm sorry."

He blew out a breath and tipped his head back, stared at the ceiling fan whirring overhead.

"How bad is it?" she said to Allison.

"Bad. If he's arrested, we need to work to get him out on bail."

"Why wouldn't he get bail?"

"Bail isn't usually given in homicide cases."

"Oh, dear lord, you'd be confined to jail?"

"Yeah, maybe you could give me some pointers about how to survive inside."

Damn, he shouldn't have said that. She was barely holding it together, and attacking her wasn't helping either of them. Even Allison was taken aback by his remark. "Look, I didn't mean to go off like that." Just seeing Tessa seemed to trigger the response. "I'm not thinking straight."

"That's not important now. Bail isn't awarded for a homicide?"

"I said, usually, Tessa. But because of Dan's reputation and his unblemished past, I think I can convince the judge to let him out."

"Can't keep the Citizen of the Year in the county jail, I'd guess," Dan said.

Allison put her hand on his shoulder. "We'll need bail money, though. A lot of it."

Tessa glanced away. "What can I do?"

"I'll need to talk to you. But Dan and I have to iron some things out first."

"Fine. Have you eaten?"

"I don't want—"

Allison stepped forward. "No, we haven't. And Dan needs some food."

"Go on into the den," his wife said. "I'll bring some sandwiches."

"Thanks."

"It's this way." He led Allison out of the room. Once he got her seated in the den, he said, "Wait here a minute, okay?"

"Uh-huh. Go talk to her."

In the kitchen, Tessa's back was to him. Her slender shoulders were slumped as she worked at the counter. Her entire body seemed to sag.

"Tessa."

She started. And then he saw her wipe her face.

"I am sorry for jumping on you. For saying those things. They're out of my mouth before I even realize what I'm saying."

"It's all right."

"Look at me."

Again, a surreptitious wipe of her face. She turned around.

"How are the girls?"

She paled. "They're fine for now. I haven't told them anything yet. I was waiting to see what happened. Nick took them out earlier." She nodded to where Allison was waiting. "Can I do anything?"

"Maybe pull together some money for bail. Check all our savings. What stocks we can cash in. And you've got your own personal account. Every bit will help."

He knew a guilty look when he saw one.

"What?"

"I—I spent all that money."

"What? Where?"

"I gave it to Frankie."

"You gave him our savings?" He couldn't believe this.

"No, no. Just what was in my account."

"And nothing else?"

She bit her lip.

"Don't you dare lie to me again."

"I hocked my pearls."

"*What?* The pearls I gave you on our wedding day?"

"Yes, I'm sor—"

He held up his hand. "Yes, I know. You're sorry."

"I'll figure out where we can get the money for bail, though. I can borrow from Janey if I have to."

"Whatever. I've got to get back to Allison."

"Go ahead. I'll bring in the food."

He'd come out here to check on her. To comfort her maybe. To take comfort from her. Now he wondered if he'd ever be able to give solace to his wife again or find it in her.

WHEN TESSA WAS FIRST SENT to prison, she'd cried herself to sleep every night. Her cellmate had sat her down at the end of the first week.

Listen, girl, you gotta toughen up, or you won't survive another week in here.

I'm so scared.

That's okay, but you need to deal better.

How do I do that?

Sonia Dunham had had a lot of advice, based on years of falling in and out of the penal system. Tessa had learned to blank her mind. Stare in the face of anyone who threatened her. Pretend she was elsewhere. She'd also made a plan for how she would make it through her three-year sentence. After a while, Tessa had found a way to cope with prison life.

Tonight, as she fixed the sandwiches, she blanked her mind. When she brought the tray into the den and found Allison and Dan, heads bent, shoulders touching, she pretended she was elsewhere. But she wasn't able to plan for the future.

She waited for Allison in the kitchen, doing meaningless chores.

Nick called to see if Dan had got back, and she gave him a rundown of what had happened. He wanted to come over, but she said Dan and Allison were busy. She was sitting at the breakfast table, listening to the nighttime sounds coming in the open window when Allison entered the room.

"Tessa?"

She looked up.

"Dan went upstairs to bed."

She didn't want to ask, but she had to know. "How bad is it?"

"It's bad. I'm sorry he made that crack about prison. But what I said about his situation is accurate."

"So they will arrest him."

"Soon, I think. You need to prepare yourself."

Tessa didn't comment. She took in Allison's perfect peach suit, setting off the thick mass of auburn hair and gray eyes Dan had once loved.

"What do you need from me?" she asked.

All lawyer now, Allison pulled her laptop out of the case and sat down. "Start from the beginning. I'll take notes. Fill me in on from when you met Hamilton until the last time you saw him."

She couldn't tell this again. She just couldn't.

"You can do this, Tessa. For Dan, you have to."

Biting back her revulsion, Tessa launched into her story. When she finished, she felt as if she was drowning in shame.

"Wow." Allison watched her. "Dan said you didn't seduce him. He said he went after you. I never believed him."

"I wouldn't have done that to another woman. Besides, I knew I wasn't the right one for him. But I fell in love with him."

Allison nodded to the computer, where she'd recorded all of Tessa's mistakes. "I'm sorry all that happened to you."

"Can you help Dan out of this?"

"Of course I can."

"He's not guilty."

"I know." Allison stood. She seemed tall, imposing and very strong. "I think it's time for me to leave. I'll be back first thing in the morning before he goes to work."

"You two won't meet at his office?"

"Ah, no. Dan doesn't want to deal with this there."

The woman closed up her computer and stuffed it into the carry case. "Try to get some rest."

Tessa walked Allison to the front door. "I appreciate what you've done so far, Allison. Especially after what happened between us all those years ago."

"No problem."

"Can I ask you something?"

"Of course."

"If it doesn't work out between me and Dan, because of what I've done, will you take him back?"

"Yes. In a heartbeat."

CHAPTER THIRTEEN

DAN WOKE UP and didn't know where he was. Light filtered in through slatted blinds over a window. An Impressionist print that Tessa loved—one of Mary Cassatt's mother and child—hung on the wall. The framed picture in the spare room had always reminded Dan of his wife. Why was he sleeping in here? In a flash, it all came back to him.

Today, he was going to be arrested for murder.

Linking his hands behind his head, Dan stared up at the whirring ceiling fan and put together in chronological order what had gone down.

First, Janey was the one who'd got the news in the *Iverton Banner* of Hamilton's release from prison. That was how Dan had discovered Janey was in collusion with Tessa about keeping Tessa's past a secret from him. And Janey knew Frankie was in town. She had lied to him outright. All the drama in the hospital after Tessa's accident took a different spin now.

Next, Tessa had bribed Hamilton with her savings

account money and pawned her pearls, the ones he'd given her as a sign of love and trust. Maybe it was appropriate that the symbol of his love for her was gone. Dan wasn't sure he could ever trust her again, and without that what chance did they have?

Finally, the kicker, the one that Dan as a husband and as a man couldn't tolerate. She didn't *know* if she would have slept with Hamilton to keep him from ruining their lives.

Yet, his protective instincts were still there, still surfaced even though he didn't want them to. In some convoluted way, he also admired her. She hadn't fallen apart. And she never, ever wavered in her belief in *his* innocence. The last thought made him ashamed, and he whipped off the covers and got out of bed. It was early morning, but he'd been asleep for hours.

Pulling on his jeans and shirt from the night before, he went in to check on Molly. She lay curled on her side, her hands under her head. The sleep of the innocent. She didn't know that today her life was going to be thrown into a tailspin. His eyes stung. What had he brought upon his children?

Nothing. Tessa had brought this travesty on all of them.

He kissed Molly's head and made his way to Sara's room.

She stirred when he entered. "Daddy?"

"Yeah, baby, it's me."

"I love you." She said the words almost in her sleep.

Pulling up the covers she'd kicked off, he whispered, "I love you, too."

He needed a shower and clean clothes, but he didn't want to go to their bedroom and face Tessa. Instead, he made his way downstairs.

So much for avoiding her.

She was in the kitchen at the table, sipping coffee, the phone pressed against her ear. "Come on, come on, Janey, answer. Please." Silence. Then a desperate, "Janey, it's Tessa. I'm sorry to bother you, but I..." Her voice caught. "I-I need you. Please, call me back." She clicked off, put the cordless receiver on the table and took another sip from the mug on the table.

"Tessa."

She started. "You scared me."

"I didn't mean to."

Crossing to the pot, he poured himself a coffee. "You were calling Janey?"

"Yes. She left town at six yesterday morning. She doesn't know anything except that Frankie came back."

"You said you needed her."

There were huge mauve circles under her eyes. "I'm fine. I didn't want her to see it on the news, if it hits over in Europe. Or for any of Brad's colleagues to find out from their connections back here."

"Ah."

"Did you sleep?"

"Yes." He scanned her outfit. She was still

wearing the pink top and capris she'd had on yesterday. "I take it you didn't?"

"Um, no, I guess not." She quickly glanced at the clock. "I'll take a nap when the kids go to school." She cleared her throat. "Dan, what should we do about them? I've been thinking about this all night. They'll have to be told before our connection to Frankie hits the paper."

"Let's see what happens today. By some miracle, it might not be as bad as we expect. Then we could spare them. Worst comes to worst, you can go get them at school."

"All right. I'm not going to work for a while. I don't even want to go out."

He watched her, thinking of the times she went out and didn't tell him. Thinking about where she went. That she saw another man, and what she did or what she was going to do with him.

"Can I…can I do anything to make this better? The tension between us is so awful I can hardly stand it."

Where she went…another man…what she was going to do with him.

Before he said anything he'd regret, he pushed away from the counter. "I'm going to shower."

"Is this how it's going to be, Dan? Because I'm not sure I can take this coldness, the ambushes like yesterday."

He hesitated.

"I'm not sure I *want* to subject myself to them anymore."

He turned abruptly.

"Have you forgotten whose fault all this is? You'll stay put and do what's expected of you until we find out the extent of this."

Her shoulders sagged, and she seemed so small and frail. "Yes, you're right. I'll stay."

TESSA ANSWERED THE PHONE a half hour later. She was cleaning up the kitchen, still dazed. Her husband's distance and cruel remarks were going to continue, and there was nothing she could do about it. She snatched up the receiver, praying it was Janey.

"Tessa, is that you?"

"Yes."

"This is Mitch Nash." His voice was strained. "I need to speak to Dan."

"Just a second." She carried the phone with her up the back stairs. Dan was finishing the knot in his tie in the mirror. "Dan, it's Mayor Nash."

He scowled in the glass. Worried, she handed him the phone. "Hello, Mayor. Yes, I know. Excuse me? Well, I *don't* know what I was thinking…. Yes, yes, of course… Yes, I'll wait it out."

When he clicked off, his hand tightened on the phone and he looked dumbstruck. "So much for innocent until proven guilty."

"What did he say?"

"That I should stay away from the office until this is settled. I guess you can't have an about-to-be-arrested felon prosecuting other criminals."

"You're not a criminal."

"That's right, you're the criminal in the family."

His words had her clutching her stomach, bending forward slightly as if she'd taken a physical blow.

"Tess, shit, I—I shouldn't have said that. I keep saying these things and I hate it. You're right about the ambushes. I need to—"

The doorbell rang.

Panic crossed Dan's face. "Already, do you think?"

She couldn't help it. Taking a step forward, she hugged him. He stiffened, didn't put his arms around her, but at least he let her hold him. "You're innocent, Dan. The justice system that you love and trust so much will determine that. I know it."

When he drew back, his face was ravaged.

The doorbell continued to peal. Dan headed downstairs, and Tessa was halfway to the first floor when he opened the door.

Allison Markham, looking like a spring flower in a green suit with a yellow blouse, stood on the doorstep. She greeted him and asked, "What happened? You look awful."

Dan drew her inside and told her about being asked to stay away from work. This time, she reached up and hugged him. Dan fell into her arms.

Without a word, Tessa went back upstairs.

AFTER HOURS IN the den with Allison, Dan headed to the kitchen to get them something to eat. From the window over the sink, he saw Tessa digging in her flower beds. It was such a homey sight, one he used to savor. He was watching her when the doorbell rang again.

"I'll get it," Allison yelled. She was expecting the police. Dan heard mumbling, then a door closing. She called out again, "Dan, come in here."

Mark Dickens was in the living room, his assistant and two uniforms behind him. "Daniel Logan, you're under arrest for the murder of Franklin R. Hamilton," Dickens said. He nodded to Nell Cumberland.

"You have the right to remain silent. Anything you say can and will be used against you…"

Dan closed his eyes and listened to the rest of the Miranda. When Cumberland was finished, one of the officers pulled handcuffs off his belt.

"Oh, my God." Tessa had come up behind him and grasped his arm. "No, don't do this."

"Tessa, please," Allison said, as if she was talking to a child who didn't quite understand the adult world.

Frowning at his officer, Dickens bit out, "Those aren't necessary, Lewis." He nodded to Dan. "I assume you'll come of your own free will.

"Yes."

"Ms. Markham, you can follow us."

Allison stepped between him and the police. "Do not say one word in their car, Dan. Do you hear me?"

"It doesn't matter."

"Of course it does!"

"Can I come with you?" Tessa asked.

"No, I'm sorry, Mrs. Logan," Dickens answered. "You have to stay here." He held up something.

"What's that?" she asked.

Allison grabbed it, read it, then showed it to Dan. "It's a search warrant."

Tessa clapped her hands over her mouth.

Looking to Allison, who nodded consent, Dan said, "Cooperate with them, Tessa. I have nothing to hide."

"Dan—"

He held up his hand. "I'll call you as soon as I can. You have to get the kids after these guys leave."

She straightened. "Of course."

If nothing else, she could still be a good mother.

KATIE GARDNER had both girls in her office when Tessa arrived. Having her house searched was a nightmare, but at least the girls weren't at home. Katie left them inside and met Tessa in the hall. "It's all over the news. I've kept them isolated."

"Yes, I know. I heard it on the way over. Thank you for protecting the girls."

"I'm so sorry, Tessa. I can't imagine what you're feeling. I know Dan could never do something like this."

Her control began to slip. "He didn't."

Katie grasped Tessa's arm. "There's more."

"More?"

"It's on the news about your past, too."

It was. All the way over she'd thought about having to tell the girls their mother had been in jail.

"I'm sorry you had such a hard life."

She knew everyone wouldn't be this kind, but she was grateful for the unexpected sympathy. "Thank you. Your concern and your regard for Molly and Sara mean a lot to me." She smiled. "I need to get the girls home."

Inside the office, her daughters were sitting on the couch in the corner coloring. They looked up when she entered.

"Mommy, honest, I didn't do anything wrong," Molly blurted out.

The comment made Tessa wince. She remembered Dan's accusation.

I won't leave my children.

Not even if you're a bad influence on them? Especially Molly.

"I know, sweetie."

The kids and her husband were victims of Tessa's past and her attempt to cover it up. The weight of her guilt was almost physical.

Sara came toward her and grabbed her hand. "Then why are you sad, Mommy?"

Tessa bit her lip. "I need to tell you why. But not here. We're going home."

"Home? But we've got school," Molly said.

"Not the rest of today." She held out her hands. "Come on, let's go."

Bidding goodbye to Katie, she left the office with the girls. As they stepped into the hall, she noticed some adults gathered near an open doorway. They turned to look at her, then one by one averted their gazes.

Tessa told herself to get used to this. She would be a pariah, now. She only hoped to God she could make this easier on the girls and Dan.

In the car, she smiled at the kids. "Put in the CD you like, Molly. We'll listen to it on the way home."

Molly had inherited Dan's instincts. "You don't like that one, Mom. You said it's annoying."

"I want to hear it today."

"Okay."

At home, Tessa led them to the family room and settled them on the couch. She sat on the heavy oak coffee table in front of them. They were quiet, sensing something bad was coming.

"I have to tell you what's happened, girls. And I want you to listen very carefully. Don't interrupt until I'm done."

They nodded. Sara slipped her hand in Molly's.

"The police have accused Daddy of something."

"What did Daddy do?" Molly asked.

"Nothing. It's a big misunderstanding. A man

Daddy was mad at died last night, and they think
Daddy had something to do with his death."

"They think Daddy *killed* somebody?" Molly's
eyes were wide with disbelief.

"They think that, honey, but it's not true."

Sara frowned. "Daddy wouldn't hurt anybody. He
says it's a sin."

"I know."

"Why do the police think he did, Mommy?"
Molly asked.

"Because Daddy had a fight with this man
before he died."

"Why?"

"Because the man wanted to hurt me. I knew him
when I was young, and he was…" She got choked
up. Frankie was crazy, but he didn't deserve to die.
"He was sick. He was trying to hurt me."

"Daddy's like your knight in shining armor, then,"
Sara stated. "Rescuing you."

Her throat closed up. *No, but he used to be.* She
could still see him as the young assistant D.A. who
strode into Chico's Diner like he could conquer the
world. "Yes, he is."

This would be the hardest. "You're also going to
hear some things about me. I was very troubled when
I was young. And I made a big mistake. I spent some
time in prison."

"What?"

"Mommy?"

She wanted to die. "It's okay to be shocked. I deserved to go, because I was in a car that killed two people." She had to tell them the details, because they'd hear it on TV, but it was one of the hardest things she'd ever had to do in her life.

Sara started to cry, and Molly visibly battled tears.

She moved to sit between them on the couch, put her arms around each of them and hugged them close. "The most important thing we can do here is support Daddy."

Molly's eyes were wide. "What does that mean?"

"Take care of him. Believe in him. Stand up for him."

They both nodded.

"People might say bad things about him to you. You have to ignore them."

"The kids at school?" Molly asked.

"Maybe."

"Will they know you went there, to that place?" Molly asked.

"Yes, and they'll say nasty things about me, too. Try to ignore that. Concentrate on Daddy, though. Defend him."

Molly's scowl was like Dan's.

"Look at me, young lady." Her daughter's confusion was evident on her face. "When something bad happens to somebody you love, you put their welfare above your own. If kids aren't nice to you, remember your loyalty is to your father."

Sara stood. "I'm going to make Dad a card. He'll like that. And one for you, Mommy."

Tessa couldn't speak around the lump in her throat.

"Are you all right, Mol?"

Her pout made the trembling of her lower lip obvious.

"Come here."

Molly threw herself into Tessa's arms. "I'm scared, Mom."

Kissing Molly's head, Tessa let her cry. "I know, sweetie. We just have to pray things will be all right for Daddy."

NICK SHOWED UP AT THE HOUSE about four in the afternoon, and Tessa suggested they sit outside, get some air. The house was closing in on her. "Do you know anything yet?" he asked.

"No. They took him away about eight this morning." She felt her throat close up. "Oh, God, Nick, they wanted to put handcuffs on him."

"I'm sorry."

Shaking off the image, she said, "I tried phoning Allison, but she hasn't returned my calls."

"I can't believe he hired her."

"I'm glad he did. She's the best in town."

He picked at a stalk of grass and toyed with it. "She's a barracuda. Their working together is not good for either Dan or you. She was none to happy when Dan chose you."

"And she was right about that, wasn't she? He should have married Allison." A tear escaped. Before she could brush it away, Nick did. The gesture was tender, and Tessa was so needy she leaned into his hand.

"Don't doubt yourself now, Tessa. When this is all over, Dan's going to regret being so cruel to you."

When this is all over, it won't matter. "He's not thinking straight."

"Aren't you upset at how he's treated you?"

"Truthfully?"

"Of course."

"He broke my heart, Nick. I'm not sure we can recover from that."

The doorbell rang, and then they heard a voice come from the kitchen. "Tessa…"

Nick threw his chair back and stood when he recognized Claire's voice. She came through the doorway leading to the backyard. "Oh, Nicholas. I didn't know you'd be here."

"Right back at you, Claire." He stepped away from the table as his mother came onto the patio, crossed to Tessa and hugged her. All the Logans wanted to touch her, except Dan.

"Thank you for calling me."

"I planned to come over to tell you in person, but

I didn't want to leave the girls, and I thought Dan might come home."

"What's the status?" Claire asked, taking a seat.

"I don't know."

"What do you mean, you don't know? Surely he's called, or at least his lawyer's called?"

"Neither one."

"I don't understand."

Perching on the benchlike top of a low brick wall around the patio, Nick crossed his arms. "It means your other son isn't the saint you always made him out to be."

"You don't think he did this awful thing?"

"Of course not! But he's being a bastard to Tessa. Striking out at her."

"Ah, a defensive trait you both have in common, then."

Tessa didn't want to deal with their problems. "Can I get you some tea, Claire?"

"Yes, dear, I'd love some."

Keeping an eye on the sullen mother and son from inside, Tessa prepared the tea, then joined her mother-in-law at the table. Nick stayed on the wall.

"Mom, aren't you mad at me? For bringing this on Dan?"

"Tessa, dear, you made a mistake. You paid for it. My son has been so happy all these years, and you've gotten him to loosen up. No, I'm not mad, and as soon as Dan gets his act together, he won't be, either."

Nick snorted. "What's this about forgiving mistakes, Claire?"

She rounded on him. "I made a mistake with you, Nicholas, and I'm sorry. I've done everything I know how to fix it. It appears I can't. But I mean what I say."

Nick didn't respond.

"Now, table this and let's help Tessa."

Together, the three of them fixed dinner and then played with the kids until Claire left.

"I'm going to the courthouse," Nick told her. "I'll find out what's going on."

Fourteen hours after Dan had been arrested, Nick called Tessa. "They've gone through the bail hearing. He can get out on $200,000 bail."

"Oh, my God."

"That's low."

"We don't have that kind of money at our fingertips." She'd checked their accounts as Dan had told her to do. "I'll have to get it from Janey. She offered it to me when she called me back."

"I've got some money he could have used. But it doesn't matter. Full bail's already been posted."

Tessa closed her eyes. "Don't tell me. By Allison Markham."

"Yep. Allison happens to have the cash on hand because she received it as part of her divorce settlement."

Tessa clutched the phone. "That's great. At least he won't have to stay in jail." All the fight drained out of her. "Is he coming home, Nick?"

"Where else would he go?"

"Take a wild guess."

CHAPTER FOURTEEN

"COME HOME WITH ME." Allison said from the driver's side of her Audi, in the courthouse parking lot. "I'll fix you a drink. Something to eat. No pressure, no having to explain things yet."

Her offer was tempting. It would be so easy to escape with her. He wondered if she was offering more than emotional solace. Probably. Did he want that? Honestly, he didn't know. "Thanks for the offer, but I can't. We haven't called Tessa all day, and she's got to be terrified about what's happened, what's going to happen."

Starting the car, Allison checked the rearview mirror and pulled out onto the street. "If you're that concerned about her feelings, then maybe you *shouldn't* go home."

"What do you mean by that?"

Allison shook her head. "I can't believe I'm saying this, but, Dan, you've been downright mean to your wife. Either you ignore her or you lash out at her."

"She brought this on me, damn it."

"Yes, she did. And believe me, I'd like nothing more than to see your marriage end and for us to have another chance together. But even I can't stand to watch you hurt her like this."

"I don't get it. You should hate Tessa for coming between you and me."

"I've never hated her. She's always had this vulnerability about her, this fragility, like a strong wind could blow her over." Allison was thoughtful. "I guess now we know why."

In the darkness of the car, broken only by the oncoming headlights, Dan realized Allison's observation was true. It was one of the reasons he'd become so protective of Tessa. He remembered teaching her how to drive and assuring her she could do it when she balked. Holding her hand through twenty-four hours of labor with Molly and telling her she was strong enough to deliver their first child. Encouraging her to complete her library science degree, insisting she was smart enough to finish the program when she wavered about her academic ability. His wife had had little enough self-confidence even before Frankie was killed.

"What did Nick say to you?" Allison's voice broke into his thoughts. "All I could hear was the shouting in the corridor when he dragged you away."

"Oh, well that was fun…"

After Dan had been released, they'd found Nick

waiting for them at the courthouse, his face flushed with anger. *Do you have any idea what you're doing to Tessa?*

Pissed at Nick's defense of Tessa once again, he'd struck out at Nick, too. *Do you have any idea what she's done to my life?*

Your life is going to right itself as soon as they find out who did this. If you keep going like you are, your marriage will never survive.

Truthfully, Nick, I'm not sure I want it to.

Then you don't deserve her.

When he told Allison the story, she frowned. "That's a bit overboard in defense of Tessa, isn't it?"

"I guess. But Nick has a thing for her."

"A thing?"

"Not in a romantic way. They've had a connection, though, right from the day he came back to Orchard Place. Sometimes, I was jealous."

"Well, as I said before, now you know why. He has a criminal background, too. He and Tessa have a lot in common."

Dan didn't like hearing Tessa called a criminal, then he remembered saying that exact thing to her. Damn, he had to get it together, at least with her.

They made the rest of the trip in silence. When Allison pulled into his driveway, he said, "Thanks for driving me home."

She surprised him by leaning over and kissing his cheek. "Don't get the wrong impression here, Dan.

I'm not giving up on you. I want you back. But I can't kick Tessa when she's down."

Ashamed that that was exactly what he'd been doing, Dan left the car and headed up the walkway. The front door was unlocked and the lights were on in the family room. He told himself he didn't need another confrontation with Tessa, but, in truth, he wanted to see her.

Obviously, she'd been waiting up for him. She lay on her side, her hands crossed over her chest, her knees drawn up. Tessa had always slept in the fetal position and never seemed relaxed in sleep. Again, now he knew why. She was holding in a big secret.

Or maybe she was afraid of being attacked. The unwelcome thought had him swaying on his feet. What had happened to his beautiful wife in prison?

Stirring, she came awake right away, as she always had. He'd thought before she was a light sleeper because of the kids. Molly was up several times a night her first year. By the time she began sleeping through, Sara was born. Dan had believed Tessa had never kicked the habit of listening for them. Now he realized the source of her easy awakening could have been a holdover from prison and what could happen if she slept too soundly.

"Dan?" She got up.

Dressed for bed in cotton, light-blue bottoms and a white T-shirt, she wrapped her arms around her waist. He could see the outline of her nipples beneath the top and the triangle of reddish curls through the flimsy material of the pants. After all she'd done, he couldn't believe he was hard at the sight of her.

"Are you all right?" she asked, her voice raw and husky.

Because he didn't like that she could still arouse him without even trying, he said more harshly than he intended, "That's a stupid question."

"Oh, I'm sorry. I guess I…"

He dropped into the chair opposite the couch, and she sat again.

"What happened?"

"They arrested me because the DNA under Hamilton's fingers and on his face matched mine."

"You told them about the fight when we went to the station yesterday."

"Yeah, but this is concrete evidence. Also, they interviewed the hotel staff. Several people heard the commotion when I kicked the door in. And the fight afterward." He studied her. "Witnesses saw you go in and out several times, too, Tessa, which is also incriminating to me."

She swallowed hard.

"One of the maids thought she saw you during the hours that Frankie died, but Dickens said your alibi is airtight."

"I never went back, Dan."

"Neither did I." He studied her. "Do you believe me, or are you just saying you do?"

"I believe you."

"Well, the police don't. They also have some other circumstantial evidence. The bartender at Zip's Café remembers Hamilton asking about you and me. Pam Mills from down the street saw me in the park talking to Hamilton."

"You put the flyer out on him. You'd hardly have done that if you were going to kill him."

"Just the opposite. It's more evidence, which may lead them to premeditated murder."

"No, oh, God, this keeps getting worse."

"It does." He shook his head. "We'll have to wait until the grand jury meets next week to see if I'm charged with manslaughter or murder one."

"I'm so sorry. I can't believe I'm responsible for all this."

He wanted to tell her it wasn't her fault. He wanted to say it was going to be all right. But, because he didn't believe either one of those things, he stood. "I'm going to bed."

"I moved your things out of the spare room."

Shocked at her suggestion, he stared into her face. "I—I can't sleep with you."

She stared at him, no emotion on her face. But she clasped her hands tightly in front of her. "I know, Dan. I put my things in the spare room. I want you to have the big bed, the private bath."

His heart ached. She'd always been this way, seeing to his comfort, putting her physical needs behind his. If there was one piece of cake left, she insisted either he or the girls eat it. If someone had to get up in the night to tend to the kids, she did it. By example, she'd taught him to be more selfless and giving.

"Thank you." He turned and trudged up the steps. Never in his life had he felt worse, not even when he'd found out his father was going to jail.

"THANKS, JANEY. I'm not going to need the money, after all." Even to her own ears, Tessa's voice was dull. And she felt listless. She hadn't wanted to get out of bed this morning.

"Why?" Her sister's voice was raw, even over thousands of miles of phone line. "I'm all set to wire it to you."

"Allison Markham paid the bail yesterday."

"So he's out?"

"Yes."

"Thank God. It's going to be all right, Tessa, I promise."

"The grand jury won't meet until next week. You don't have to fly back from London tomorrow."

"I do!" Janey's voice held a note of panic now. "I do."

"But you should stay there for Brad."

"No, I'm coming home to help you."

Tessa shook her head. "At least try to enjoy the dinner and festivities for him."

"Don't worry about me. Hang on, and I'll be there long before the indictment."

"Thanks. I love you. How did I get so lucky to have a sister like you?"

Tessa made her way to the laundry room. Just putting one foot in front of the other and doing routine tasks was difficult. She'd told the girls they couldn't go to school today. The whole community now knew what had happened, and she wouldn't subject her daughters to the other kids' cruelty. They only had a few days left in the school year anyway. Molly had been upset that she couldn't go to the picnic, but in the end both kids had gone back to bed. Two hours later, Dan was still sleeping, too. At least she thought he was. He hadn't come out of the bedroom in any case.

Tessa put in a load of white clothes and was folding the towels from the dryer when she saw through the laundry room window an unfamiliar car pull up. She was stunned when the kids' principal got out the driver's side—and Molly climbed out of the back. Nick drove in right behind them.

That shocked her out of her malaise. Hurrying out the side door, Tessa met them on the blacktop. "What's going on?" Katie clutched Molly at her side. Her little girl's face was buried in Katie's skirt, and she wouldn't look at Tessa.

Nick took Tessa's hand. "Molly snuck out and went to school. She wanted to go to the picnic."

"Oh, no."

Tessa knelt down in front of her daughter. "Baby, are you okay?"

"Don't be mad."

"I'm not."

Molly, her wild child, her tough little tomboy, burst into tears and threw herself into Tessa's arms. She sobbed as if her insides were coming out.

"Shh. Shh." Tessa rubbed Molly's back.

"The kids said Daddy's a murderer."

"Oh, sweetie, I told you Daddy's innocent. And we have to support him."

"Sammy Carter said you were a criminal, too, Mommy. And that Daddy's problems are your fault. She said I can't go to her birthday party."

Tessa felt the blood drain from her face. Her knees were wobbly when she stood. "Thanks for bringing her home."

"You're welcome. I'm sorry. I wish I could have headed this off."

Tessa glanced at Nick, who added, "Katie called and asked me what she should do. I said I'd meet her here to see if I could help in any way."

"What's going on out here?" Dan came into the sunlight, wearing jeans and a dark T-shirt. He must have gotten some sleep because he looked better.

Tessa couldn't bear telling him what had happened to their child. "I think I'll let them fill you in." She nodded to Katie. "Thanks again."

Tessa left with Molly. She held her little girl's hand all the way upstairs, where Sara joined them. Tessa explained once again what she'd done to bring this down on them. She reiterated all she'd told them yesterday on the couch, not defending herself, but trying to make this as easy on them as possible. Once she got them settled with some books, she went to the spare bedroom, put sneakers on and crept down the back stairwell.

She escaped into the wild area behind their house where they sometimes went back to picnic. Or to be alone. Once she and Dan had made love on a blanket under the stars. When she reached the cleared area, she dropped down on the hard ground, drew up her knees and buried her face in her arms.

And wept for what she'd done to Dan and to her children.

DAN FOUND HER behind the house after following the sound of her wrenching sobs. He stood for a long time, torn about what he should do, but her misery was so great, she didn't notice him. Finally, he knelt in front of her. "Tessa?"

She didn't look up at him right away. But when she did, her face told him everything he needed to know. She'd had about all she could take, had finally snapped. "Honey, stop."

She buried her face back in her arms. The crying resumed.

"Tessa, please, stop."

He couldn't stand it anymore. It was awkward, with him on his knees, but he drew her into his arms. He thought she might push him away, resist after how he'd treated her, but she clung to his T-shirt, her face in his chest. And though he didn't think it was possible, she cried harder.

He rubbed circles on her back. "Shh. Shh."

"I can't believe…I can't believe I've done this to you and to my children. I can't believe it."

He didn't know what to say so he drew her closer and cradled her to his heart. It felt right to hold her.

Then, he was hit with a stunning realization.

If he hadn't struck out at her, hadn't distanced her, they could have helped each other through this nightmare. He could have supported her and eased her guilt, prevented this meltdown, and she could have given him the comfort and hope he needed to face the legal ramifications of Hamilton's death.

Now, under the canopy of trees, on this beautiful day, the sight of the woman he loved collapsed with grief made him more ashamed of himself than he'd ever been in his life. He'd let her down and by doing that made everything she had to endure so much worse.

After a long time, she settled down. For a while, she let him hold her, then pulled away and stood. So did he. She pushed back her hair and wiped her face with her hands. "I'm sorry. I promised myself I wouldn't do this. Poor Molly and Sara. Dan, what are we going to do about them?"

This he could help with. This they could tackle together, like they'd always done with problems. "Take one day at a time. Try to make things livable for them. Maybe my mother can take them away for a while. I know she wants to help."

"Where are they now?"

"Nick's kids came over. The ones who seem close to you."

The anger at everything he hadn't known about her threatened to come back, but this time, he was able to keep it in check. As he should have done all along.

"Since the fair, Sara had been singing Chelsea's praises and Molly's taken a shine to Beth. They were with Nick when Katie called him, so they came over to see if they could distract the girls."

"How sweet."

"Are you going to be okay?"

She nodded like a little girl, trying to convince her parents she was all right when she didn't believe it herself.

"Ready to go back?"

"Yes."

She was still trembling, but she held her head up and straightened her shoulders. He wanted to take her hand, but he wasn't sure he could make the overture, wasn't sure she wanted him to.

When she stumbled on the path, though, he grabbed for her hand. Not only did she let him take it, but she leaned in to him. Together, they made their way back home.

CHAPTER FIFTEEN

NICK WAS STILL AT THE HOUSE when Tessa and Dan came in from the backyard. Katie Gardner had left to go back to school. With a few words for his brother Dan closeted himself in the den to prepare for his meeting with Allison. Nick and Tessa shared mugs of coffee in the breakfast nook while the four girls were upstairs.

After the catharsis in the backyard, and Dan's support, Tessa felt as if she might be able to handle what came next. She didn't know if Dan had got past striking out at her, but right now she'd take what she could get.

"Thanks for bringing Chelsea and Beth, Nick."

"When I went upstairs, they were fiddling with each other's hair and doing makeup. It wasn't pretty." His blue eyes gleamed with pride, though there were grooves around his mouth. Dan's arrest had been hard on everyone.

Despite the circumstances, Tessa chuckled. "How's Chelsea feeling?"

"She bounced right back. She said you were a godsend." He sipped his coffee. "Thanks for being with her through the miscarriage."

"I wanted to be there."

He shook his head. "You were in the midst of your own crisis, and still you went running to Chelsea when she needed you."

"Of course I went. Anyone would have done the same thing."

He snorted. "No, they wouldn't, but the very fact that you don't know that makes you even more special." He hesitated. "And some good deeds pay off."

"I wish I didn't have the alibi, Nick. I wish they'd accused me instead of Dan."

The doorbell rang, and they heard Dan answer it, heard the low murmur of conversation. Allison Markham had arrived. Nick squeezed her fingers in support, as if he sensed how bad it made Tessa feel to have Allison and Dan working so closely.

"Hi, all," Allison said as she and Dan came into the kitchen together. Her gaze zeroed in on Tessa's and Nick's hands, still clasped on the table. Tessa drew hers back as if she'd done something wrong.

Again, Allison was dressed to the nines in a rose suit, with a light pink shell underneath. She wore the kind of heels Tessa hadn't squeezed into since she was twenty. She was intelligent. And competent. For the hundredth time, Tessa wondered why Dan had ever chosen her over this remarkable woman.

"There's some good news," Dan said. "And some bad news."

"I wanted to tell you all together." Allison nodded to Nick. "You, especially."

"Can I get you coffee?" Tessa asked, already rising.

"Sure."

She picked up Nick's cup to refill it and poured some for Allison. Dan took a chair on the other end of the table.

When they were all seated, Allison folded her hands around the mug. "I've had some private investigators working around the clock for three days. They found some information that might help Dan's case."

"Why would you be doing that and not the police?" Nick asked.

"The police think they have the case all wrapped up," Dan answered. "They don't need to find other suspects."

"What did you find out, Allison?" Tessa asked.

"Ike Summers, the husband of the woman you—" she glanced away "—who was killed in the accident, is missing."

"Missing?" Nick frowned. "From where?"

"He still lives in Iverton, but he left town a week ago. My people nosed around. The neighbors and his coworkers said he'd been acting odd since Frankie was released. He grumbled a lot about Frankie not paying for his sins before he disappeared. No one has seen him since."

"That poor man. He lost so much. I can understand why Frankie's release would hit him hard."

"In any case, I have some contacts at the D.A.'s office in Ohio who are going to see if he left a paper trail."

"What are you looking for?" Nick asked.

"For one thing—" Dan said "—they might be able to find credit-card slips for gas or food or hotels. If he headed this way, those would show it."

"If so, there would be another prime suspect," Allison added.

Dan smiled at his lawyer. "Very astute to think of this, Allison."

Tessa swallowed hard at the admiration he showed his ex-fiancée.

"Don't thank me yet. It's just a lead. But it is good news."

Rising, Dan refilled his coffee mug. "What's the bad news?"

"I have another suspect, and I thought I might as well get it out in the open now."

"Who?" Tessa asked.

She faced Nick. "You."

Dan slapped his mug on the countertop. "What the hell are you talking about?"

Tessa looked across the table. "Nick?"

Nick's eyes narrowed on Allison, but he kept silent.

Dan marched over to Allison. "Nick couldn't have done something like this. What the hell would make you suspect my brother?"

"You want to tell them, Nick, or should I?"

"You're thorough." Nick's voice was clipped. "When I left Orchard Place at seventeen, I got in more trouble than either of you know."

"How much trouble?" Dan asked.

"I spent time in jail for using drugs." Here he glanced at Allison. "And I beat a guy up; he was in a coma for a long time."

"Oh, Nick." Tessa touched his arm.

"That's not all. The guy was stalking a woman I was involved with."

"It doesn't matter. I know you couldn't kill anyone." Dan's defense of his brother was quick. And adamant. Tessa remembered that first morning when they'd found out Frankie was dead. *Did you do this*?

Some of Dan's comfort this morning wore off.

"Well," Allison said. "I don't know Nick didn't do it. Not unless he has an alibi when Hamilton was killed." She asked, point-blank, "Where were you, Nick, after Dan left you that day?"

Nick ran his finger around the rim of his mug. He didn't speak for a long time. "I'm sorry, I can't tell you that."

"WHAT THE HELL is going on, Allison?" Dan asked her when they were alone in the den.

"Just what I said. Your brother could have killed Frankie. He had as much of an opportunity as you had."

"He didn't kill anyone."

Allison frowned. She'd worn her hair in a thick braid today, and she fussed with the end of it. "How can you be so sure?"

"He's my brother. I know him. I know he couldn't have killed anybody."

"His past behavior indicates a violent personality."

"Which you checked into. Why did you do that, anyway?"

"Because any capable defense attorney, given a solid case against her client, like yours by the way, would investigate all possible leads. Nick's a prime suspect." She watched him. "Hell, so is Janey Christopher. Everybody in town knows how close she and Tessa are. I'd guess she'd do anything for her sister. I intend to question her as soon as she gets back."

"That's ridiculous. Janey can't even kill a spider."

"I'm following every lead I have, Dan. That includes your brother."

"So Nick was in more trouble than I knew. But that was a long time ago. He went to school, got two college degrees and is now helping kids. I admire him."

"Interesting."

"What?"

"You'd give Nick a second chance and not Tessa."

"I don't want to discuss Tessa."

Because Allison was dead-on. Now, he knew he'd been wrong to suspect Tessa, wrong about a lot of things. It was like a switch clicked on in his brain out in the woods this morning.

"What would be Nick's motive, Allison? And don't say he'd kill for me. I don't buy that."

"Maybe not for you."

"Excuse me?"

"Dan, you are so blind. You haven't seen what's been under your nose for a long time."

"What?"

"Nick's in love with Tessa. He'd do anything for her. Even commit murder to protect her."

"You're crazy. He's not in love with my wife."

"You've told me things that indicate he is. And I'm sure you don't know the half of what's gone on. Watching them together convinced me. Hell, Dan, she refilled his coffee without even asking if he wanted it. And they were holding hands when we walked into the kitchen. As a matter of fact, he's always touching her."

"He's affectionate."

"Bullshit."

"This isn't happening. You honestly think Tessa's been having an affair, as well as keeping things from me?"

"No, I don't think she's been having an affair. She's not the type. And I doubt she returns his feelings. But my gut instinct tells me Nick's head over heels."

Everybody's a little bit in love with her.

You don't deserve her.

If she was my wife, I'd do anything to protect her from all this.

"I can't take in what you're saying."

"Well, you'd better. Because your brother could be guilty of murder."

Dan shook his head.

"Then why won't he say where he was?"

"I have no idea. But I'm going to find out."

Dropping into his desk chair, Dan laid his head back on the smooth leather. His glance swept the desk, taking in the Web site he'd been scanning. He wondered where Nick had gone to prison. And what else he didn't know about his brother. He wondered if Tessa knew about Nick. He wondered if Nick loved her.

"Until I talk to Nick, I want you to put your investigation of him on hold, Allison."

"No. I won't have my hands tied. If you want to run this defense, I'll bow out. But I won't share it with you." She stood, and when he started to speak, held up her hand. "Don't say anything now. You're reacting out of emotion. Think it over and call me. I recommend you let me do my job. I may be your only hope."

Dan stayed in his den after she'd gone. About an hour later, Tessa appeared at his doorway. "Nick left," she said. If possible she looked worse than she had out in the woods.

"Why didn't he say goodbye to me? I wanted to talk to him about Allison's accusation."

"I guess he thought she was still here. We went upstairs and visited the kids, so we didn't hear her leave."

"Where did he go?"

"He wouldn't say." She came into the room and stood in front of the desk, her hands folded across her stomach. "He didn't do it, Dan."

"Of course he didn't. Do you know where he was that day?"

"He won't say."

"Well, if he won't tell you, he won't tell anybody."

"What does that mean?"

"Allison thinks he's in love with you."

"Allison's wrong. We're close. We've always been. I feel a connection with Nick."

"I know."

"You can see why, I guess."

This time, he didn't strike out at her, he didn't want to.

For some reason, she wouldn't leave it alone. "Aren't you going to make the obvious conclusion—about what we have in common? That Nick and I are both ex-convicts?"

"I deserve that, I guess. I haven't been kind to you." He looked out his window, which faced the woods. "I know I should have handled all this better. I will, from now on, Tess."

She shrugged. "None of that matters." He hated the resignation in her voice. And was afraid it meant that it was too late to make up for what he'd done.

She picked up a picture of her and Dan, taken at a cottage on Keuka Lake. They'd been married a year. Tessa had just gotten pregnant with Molly, and they were blissfully happy.

"Allison told me I've been behaving badly."

"She probably thinks it will hurt the case somehow. Let's table this. I'm…" Her words trailed off. She frowned at something on the desk.

He tracked her gaze to see what she was looking at. It was his computer screen. Shit!

Tessa's eyes blurred with tears. It wasn't that big a deal. She didn't know why this affected her so much. Maybe because it was the last straw in a series of attacks she wasn't strong enough to withstand. Allison was, after all, right about what she'd said. With the exception of their time together this morning, Dan had treated her like dirt.

With a calm that comes from hitting bottom, she asked, "What are you looking for, Dan?"

"Nothing. I—"

She moved in closer to the computer. "Federal Prison Camp Assault Statistics." She shook her head, and her gaze caught on papers that were strewn across the desk's surface. The headline on one printed from the Internet stood out: Dawson Federal Prison Camp. She picked it up and scanned its contents. "I see."

"No, no, you don't."

Raising her eyes, she was surprised to find him so emotional. "Of course I do. You were checking out the prison where I served time." She nodded to the screen. "You were hunting for statistics on assaults in prison camps." She shuddered. "Did you find what you were looking for?"

"Tess—"

"Did you?"

"Tessa, please."

"Did you?"

He wouldn't answer her, but his expression was as guilty as hell.

"Why didn't you just ask me, Dan?" Now, *her* tone wasn't so nice, but she didn't care.

She got no response. Because there was no defense for this.

"You want to know if I was raped in prison, don't you? You want to know the extent of how tainted your wife is."

"No." Despite his protest, she recognized the confirmation on his face. She sucked in a breath. *Why* did this hurt so much? It wasn't the worst thing he'd done to her. Closing her eyes, she swallowed back the bile in her throat.

He circled the desk and grasped her by the arms, as if he knew what a big deal this was, too. "Tessa, it isn't that. At least not how you interpreted it."

She shrank back from him. "Don't touch me."

"Mrs. Logan?" Tessa registered the voice but couldn't seem to pinpoint it. She felt like she was suffocating.

Dan turned to the doorway. "Hi, Chelsea. Is everything all right with the girls?"

"Yes." She eyed Tessa. "Mrs. L? What's wrong? You're white as a sheet."

"I'm fine. What do you need?"

"Beth and I want to take Sara and Molly on a picnic since they missed the school one today. We'd go over to the park, and no kids'll be around yet. Would that be okay?"

"Of course. It's a terrific idea."

"Are you sure you're all right?"

"I'm fine." She gave Chelsea a phony smile. "Come on, I'll help you pack a lunch."

TESSA KEPT HER distance from Dan all through the afternoon. He'd tried to talk to her, but she managed to slip away each time. And besides, what could he say? He had been doing precisely what she said—scrutinizing Dawson Federal Prison Camp, trying to piece together what might have happened to her there. But not for the reasons she accused him of. When it hit him what could have happened to her in that place, he'd felt bad for her. Not repulsed, like she thought. Just horrified at what she might have gone through.

After he'd tried calling Nick several times, he'd gone out looking for his brother but couldn't find him. So he came back and went for a run. The exercise helped clear his head, which was unfortunate, because as he pounded the pavement he thought about Tessa and how she'd behaved so well during this ordeal.

Even in the midst of all the trouble, she'd tried to see to his welfare, fixing him meals, suggesting he sleep in. Today, when he went to their bedroom to get his running clothes, the sheets had been changed, the bed made and the bathroom straightened.

While he'd been battering her with insults, ignoring her, making her feel like hell, she'd cleaned the room where he was sleeping. That had sent him running.

He let himself into the house about four. He wondered if the girls were back; there was a strange car in the driveway, and it didn't belong to the two teens who'd flocked to Tessa's aid. Maybe one of Tessa's friends or coworkers had come to offer her moral support. There had been a steady stream of calls, he knew, from neighbors and friends who had asked if they could help. But in the kitchen, he was surprised to see Katie Gardner sitting with Tessa.

"Did something else happen at school?" he asked.

Tessa's eyes were blank when she looked up at him. "No, Katie wants to talk to us. She waited for you to get back before she'd say why she was here."

Wiping the sweat from his face with a paper towel, he crossed the room and sat down at the table. "What is it, Katie?"

Katie's pretty complexion flushed. "I talked to Nick earlier."

"Nick?"

"Yes. He came to school to warn me."

"About what?"

"That Allison Markham is investigating where he was between the hours of three and seven on the day Frankie Hamilton was killed."

"Why would he come to you?" Tessa asked.

"I didn't know you knew Nick that well," Dan added.

Her laugh was sad. "Oh, I know him well." She twisted the wedding band on her left hand. "I'm Nick's alibi. He was with me that afternoon."

"The entire time?" Tessa asked. "Then why wouldn't he tell Allison?"

"Because we were over in Clarence…at The Niagara Motel. For four hours. He dressed there to go to the Citizen of the Year dinner." She shrugged. "He was trying to protect me and my marriage. You see, I've been having an affair with Nick for months."

CHAPTER SIXTEEN

FOR THE NEXT TWO DAYS, Dan and Tessa walked around like robots, treating each other with polite concern, talking only when necessary. At Dan's suggestion, Claire had taken the girls to see her sister in New York City. At least her children were away from the scandal and being cared for. Tessa could barely take care of herself, and Dan wasn't in much better shape. The waiting was hard on both of them.

She was in the kitchen putting away groceries, when Dan walked in from his second run of the day. He crossed to the refrigerator and took out a bottle of water.

"How was your run?" Tessa asked, trying to make conversation. Sometimes the strain between them was so great, it was a tangible presence in the room.

"It helped."

He leaned against the counter, sweat dripping off his face, his gray shirt soaked. Mid-June had turned blistering hot. She rinsed some glasses in the sink and put them in the dishwasher, feeling her own clothes cling to her clammy body. After a moment, he said, "You look different."

Warm, she lifted the hair off her neck. "I let my hair dry on its own instead of using the blow dryer."

"I always liked it this way."

Past tense. They were both making slips like that. As if their relationship was over, as if it had died in that hotel room with Frankie.

"You wouldn't have if you knew why I straightened it. I used to wear it like this when I was young."

"Ah." He sipped his water. "Did you go to yoga?"

"Yes. It felt great to be back."

Tessa could feel Dan watching her. He did that a lot now. Was he seeing her in a new light or looking for more flaws, wondering just how soiled she was?

"How did he find you there that day? When he hit you?"

These kinds of questions were killing her. "He must have followed me."

"Were you scared?"

She gripped the edge of the counter and snapped, "Of course I was scared."

"Tessa, listen—"

"Don't. I can't take much more of your probing, your analyzing what happened to me in the past few weeks." Thinking of the Web sites, she added, "Or in the past."

"I am only concerned about what you went

through." He hesitated, then finished. "And I deeply regret not being there to help you."

Another tense silence. Finally, she asked, "Is Allison coming back tonight?" His lawyer had been there all morning, huddled with Dan in the den. After Nick's alibi checked out, Allison had put even more people on the search to locate Ike Summers.

"Yes, I expect her around supper time."

"Fine. I'm going over to Janey's. She called from Atlanta and said she'd be landing about six." Tessa didn't know why she added, "I don't want to watch you and Allison together again tonight." She guessed she was through hiding her reactions.

"You say that as if you think there's something going on between us."

"No, I don't think there is. Yet." She untied the dish towel around her waist, tossed it on the counter and started to brush past him.

He put his hand on her arm to prevent her from leaving. "What do you mean by *yet?*"

"I mean that as soon as this is over and you and I split, I'm sure you'll have a nice life with her."

"Assuming I'm cleared, is that what you think is going to happen?"

"Yes, Dan, I do."

"So there's no chance for us?"

Her eyes filled. "You know there isn't. One of us should say the words aloud. I've done irreparable damage to you and your reputation. And you've…"

His hand tightened on her arm. "Tess, talk to me."

"You've made it clear that I repulse you. What's happened to me in the past, at the very least what I *did* in the past. I'm not who you thought I was, Dan. It's okay, I can live with that. But I can't live with your distaste on a daily basis. Besides, if you stay with me it would be out of a sense of responsibility, and I couldn't bear that after what we've had together."

"You've got it all wrong, sweetheart."

She clapped her hand over her mouth. "Oh, please don't do that. Call me that. Pretend you don't feel disdain for me when a few days ago you were on the computer trying to find out…"

A knock cut her off; they heard the front door open.

"Allison is just walking into the house now?" she asked.

Shaking his head, Dan pushed away from the counter. "Not that I know of."

"Tessa…" Her sister's voice came from the foyer.

"It's Janey! She's back!" Tessa rushed out of the kitchen and found Janey and Brad in the foyer.

When Janey saw her, she threw herself into Tessa's arms. "Oh, honey, I'm so sorry."

Tessa held on tight. She hadn't realized how scared she'd been. Maybe Janey had been right on the phone. Maybe things would be better now that she was back. She hugged her sister for a long time, then over her shoulder saw that Brad was watching them. His eyes were troubled—and moist. Alarm came on the heels of her relief. What would Tessa do if Brad turned on her, too?

Janey pulled back. "I have to talk to you."

Brad slid his arm around Janey. "*We* have to talk to you." He kissed Janey's hair and nodded to the living room. "Come on, let's sit in here."

They both seemed to notice Dan for the first time. Janey started to cry again at the sight of him. Brad said, "Hi, buddy."

"Hi, you two."

"We have a lot to tell you." Keeping Janey tucked in his arm, Brad led her into the family room and they sat together on the couch. Janey held his hand in a death grip. Tessa and Dan took the chairs.

"Tessa, I don't know how to…"

Brad leaned his head close to hers. "Just get it out, love."

With a quick glance at Dan, Janey blurted out, "I killed Frankie Hamilton."

DAN COULDN'T HAVE heard right. "What did you say, Janey?"

"Oh, Dan, oh, God, I'm sorry. I killed Frankie."

"This isn't true." Tessa crossed the room and knelt in front of her sister. "Janey, you're trying to make everything all right again, like you always do, like you said you would when you got home. But you can't make a fake confession to save Dan."

"That's not what I'm doing."

"Of course it is. I appreciate the gesture, but—" Tessa stopped mid-sentence and looked at Brad. "Why would you let her do something like this, Brad?"

"Because it's true." He drew in a breath. "I'm sorry we've caused all this trouble. Janey wanted to tell you on the phone, but I insisted she do it in person."

Dan had gone cold when it began to sink in that Janey's confession was genuine. A million questions formed in his muddled brain. "How long have you known, Brad?"

"She told me after the reception in London. She didn't want to spoil the honor for me."

"Spoil things for *you?*" He couldn't take it all in. "What about us? She could have told us a week ago and avoided this—"

"I know. She should have. She wasn't thinking clearly."

Tessa sank to the floor and buried her head in her hands. "No, I can't have caused this, too."

The sight of his wife weeping for her sister kicked Dan in the gut.

Jumping up from the couch, Janey dropped to the floor and drew Tessa's hands away from her face. "You didn't cause this, honey. I did."

"I've ruined everybody's life."

"Let us tell you what happened, okay?" Brad said.

Dan watched the scene as if it was a movie, happening to someone else.

Janey cleared her throat. "After you left on that Tuesday, I got together some money and went to the Heritage House before dinner. I thought I could bribe Frankie into leaving town."

"Janey, I told you he was irrational."

"I know. I didn't realize how irrational until I got there. He thought I was you, thought I'd come back to be with him."

"You must have been so scared."

"He came after me. I kept saying I wasn't you, but he didn't believe it. So then I pretended I *was* you and told him things were over between us." She glanced at Brad, who nodded. "Then he attacked me. He said if he couldn't have me, *you* really, then no one could."

"Oh, my God."

"I grabbed the nearest thing—a lamp—when he came at me, and I hit him. I thought I just dazed him. He fell on the bed, moaning but coherent. There wasn't much blood, so I figured he was okay. I called 911 just in case."

"That explains the maid who thought she saw Tessa at the scene of the crime." Now that it was sinking in, Dan's anger was building. "You could have told us the night of the Citizen dinner, since it was self-defense."

"I didn't know he was dead until the day after I got to London."

"You expect us to believe that?"

"I do." Tessa brushed back Janey's hair. "You must have been terrified."

"Especially when I talked to you on the phone."

"You could have told her then," Dan said. "So much of this could have been avoided." So much of what Dan had brought on them by his reprehensible behavior wouldn't have happened. Not that any of that was Janey's fault.

"I know I should have told you on the phone. I panicked. But I never expected them to accuse you, Dan. They gave you the Citizen of the Year award. I thought…I don't know what I thought. By the time I realized what had happened to you, I figured for sure you'd be exonerated. Then I waited…" Her eyes were wide and empty. "It doesn't matter. I'm so sorry, Tessa."

"You're sorry?" Tessa asked.

All right, this is better, Dan thought. *Now she's angry, as she should be.*

"I'm the one who's *sorry*. This never would have happened if I hadn't gotten myself involved with Frankie to begin with."

Dan bolted off the chair. "Your sister has ruined our lives, Tessa."

Tessa looked up at Dan, then extricated herself from Janey and stood. "No, Dan, *I'm* responsible for all this."

"Janey killed him."

"Stop it!" Brad stood and drew Janey up from the

floor. "Leave my wife alone. She was scared. She got confused. She didn't know what to do."

"She should never have done this to her sister."

Brad's face reddened. "I know you're angry about what's happened to your wife. But do *not* say another word about mine or I swear to God, Dan, I'll deck you."

Tessa stepped between them. "Calm down, both of you." She faced Dan. "I won't let you do to Janey what you did to me. I deserved your contempt, she doesn't. She was trying to protect me."

He took a couple of steps back. "Look, I…" He sighed. "I'm sorry I lost my temper. I'm in shock, but I shouldn't have said those things, Janey."

Brad reached around Tessa to put his hand on Dan's shoulder. "I know. We're all sorry. Let's sit down and talk about how we're going to tell the police. I'm so worried about her I can't—"

The doorbell rang. "That's Allison Markham," Tessa said. "She was coming over to work on Dan's defense."

"Do you think she can help us?" Brad asked.

Us.

"Yes, I think so. She's done a thorough job handling Dan's case. She'll know how to direct us." Tessa hugged her sister. "No matter what, Janey, I'll always be here for you. And I don't blame you."

Brad hugged Tessa.

The sight of the three of them supporting one

another upset Dan. Tessa had no animosity toward her sister. And Brad had stood by his wife without reservation. Right from the outset, he'd done for Janey what Dan had never once done for Tessa.

As Dan let Allison into the house, he was well aware of one merciless fact. He could never make up to Tessa for how he'd behaved in the past few weeks.

"HOW DO WE KNOW it was self-defense, Dan?" Karen Jackson, his assistant D.A. asked. "Maybe Jane Christopher *did* kill Hamilton to protect her sister."

Though he wasn't back at work in an official capacity, Dan had visited the office today to talk to Karen. The charges against him had been dropped yesterday morning when Janey had confessed to the police. The mayor had called to say he was glad Dan had been exonerated and he could go back to work anytime. But Dan wouldn't be handling this case, of course, and he wasn't ready to jump into another, so he'd leave after this meeting.

"That's why I'm here, Karen. There was a maid who thought she saw Tessa in the hotel at the time of the murder."

"I saw something about that in the police report. The investigators dismissed her testimony because Tessa's alibi was airtight."

"And because they got a lot of crank calls on this murder."

"I'll check out the identity of this woman."

"You should also interview the hotel staff again. Someone else may have heard or seen something that would support Janey's contention of self-defense."

"I'll get right on it. For what it's worth, I hope Jane is innocent of anything but self-defense."

"So do I."

"How's Tessa taking this?"

Dan didn't know. "She's upset."

"It must have been terrible for her. First, she had to worry about you. Now her sister. I couldn't deal with it if I were her. I guess she's pretty strong."

She was. Over the past two days, Dan had witnessed a side of Tessa he'd never seen before. She'd been unswervingly supportive of her sister, not leaving Janey's side, moving into their guest room, spending every waking moment with the Christophers. Brad had sung Tessa's praises when he'd called to see how Dan was faring.

"You okay, Dan?"

Just feeling like a shit. "Yeah, I'm going to stop at my office to get a few things, then I'm heading out."

"When are you coming back to work?"

"Soon."

Once in his office, he called the Christophers' house. The answering machine picked up. He left yet another message. "Tessa, please, call me back. I know you're busy with Janey, but take a few minutes to—"

"Dan, hello?" She'd picked up and sounded out of breath.

"Hi. Did I catch you at a bad time?"

"I made Janey go for a walk with me. Listen, I'm sorry I haven't returned your calls. It's been hectic. Brad's trying to deal with the fallout with his practice and the grant people. He's also trying to spend as much time as he can with the boys."

"Are you well? Eating? Sleeping?" he asked her.

"As much as can be expected."

"Tessa, can I see you? Just for an hour or so?"

A long pause. "No, not now. Let me get Janey through this."

"Sweetheart, I know I've behaved badly. I can't quite believe how badly, now that I have some perspective. Could we at least discuss it?"

"Maybe after everything is settled with Janey."

"You aren't coming home until then?"

"Home?" She said the word as if it was foreign to her. "No, not until the girls return. I'll move back in then. I have to go now. Take care of yourself."

"Tessa, wait—"

But she'd hung up.

"What did you expect?" Dan glanced over to see Nick in the doorway. Dressed like Dan in jeans and a golf shirt, he leaned against the doorjamb.

"Don't start. I feel bad enough."

"My guess is you're going to feel a lot worse before you feel better."

"Why, do you know something?"

Nick sauntered in and dropped into a chair. "Pretty much what I gathered by hearing your end of the conversation just now on the phone." Nick watched him. "I told her she should see you, by the way."

"You've talked to her? She said she wouldn't..." He sighed. "I get it. She won't see *me*."

"I'm sorry, Dan."

"How often have you seen her?"

"A couple of times. So have my girls. Chelsea even went over to Janey's to run errands for them and do some chores."

"So I'm the one cut out of all this."

Nick raised his eyebrows.

"Never mind. I'm done with that kind of self-absorption. How are *you*?"

"I'm hanging in. I hear Claire took the girls out of town. Couldn't stand another scandal, could she?"

"She was trying to protect my children, drove them down to visit Aunt Millie. Give her a break."

"Ain't gonna happen, buddy. I will, however, encourage Tessa to give you one."

It killed him to ask, but he did. "When will you see her again?"

"Tonight. I'm invited for dinner. She thought I might distract Janey. Brad's taking the boys out fishing on the lake."

"Then it'll be just you and Tessa."

"And a falling-apart Janey. What's going to happen to her, Dan?"

"I don't know. She'll be arraigned soon. I hope they find enough evidence that she acted in self-defense before then."

"I do, too."

Dan watched his brother. "Nick, I never asked you about Katie Gardner. What's going on there?"

"Nothing, now. Her husband has friends in the police department. It got around that she was my alibi."

"I'm surprised you'd hook up with a married woman."

He shrugged, but his face was drawn. "Me, too. It just kind of happened. Joe Gardner travels eighty percent of the time. Katie was lonely. I was lonely. She's a nice woman. I hope I haven't screwed up her life too much."

"I know the feeling," Dan mumbled.

After Nick left, Dan sat back in the chair. Looking around the office, he remembered thinking how he might never get to work here again, how he might lose all this.

And how important that had seemed. Now, he'd have his career back. But what else?

TESSA WAITED OUTSIDE the grand jury hall with Brad. No one was allowed in the inner sanctum to watch the proceedings. Janey's lawyer, Mike Holt, one of Allison Markham's associates, would present their case to the panel of sixteen, who would decide if Janey would be indicted for murder.

Her brother-in-law paced the corridor. Alone with Tessa, he let himself voice his fears.

"We have to have faith, Brad."

"In what? A system that would accuse someone like Dan? A system that might indict my wife for protecting herself?"

"Yes. They're going to believe the testimony of the maid."

At Dan's urging, Karen had found the maid, and she'd told her story all over again. She saw what she thought was the woman who'd been in and out of the hotel for a week, come to Frankie's room at about four o'clock on the day of his death. From the corridor, she'd heard the woman inside cry out. And she'd heard a loud crash. It hadn't sounded right, but sometimes people got crazy during sex, she thought, so she'd gone into a room to clean it. The maid didn't know anything bad had happened.

Brad sat beside her. "How are you holding up?"

"Okay. I miss the girls."

"Only the girls?"

She gave him a small smile. "Dan, too. Of course I miss him."

"Speak of the devil…"

Tessa looked up to find Dan standing a few feet away. She hadn't seen him in five days. The girls were coming back tomorrow from their vacation with Claire, and Tessa knew she had to go home, but she thought she'd be prepared for confronting him. She wasn't. He looked big, but breakable, and so sad it hurt to see his face.

"I hope it's all right that I came."

Brad stood and shook his hand. "Sure it is."

Tessa said, "Hello, Dan."

"Do you know anything about all this?" Brad asked.

"Only that Karen Jackson believes Janey's story. The trick will be if Holt can convince the grand jury."

"It's a good sign that the assistant D.A. believes her, though, isn't it?"

Squeezing Brad's shoulder in support, Dan gave him a hopeful smile. "Yeah, Brad, it is."

Running a hand over his bald head, Brad sighed. "I don't know what I'd do without Janey."

Tessa murmured words of encouragement.

Brad glanced at her, then at Dan. "I'll give you two some time alone." He walked down the corridor and took a seat within view of the grand jury door.

Dan stood in front of Tessa. Up close, she noticed the lines around his eyes, the strain etched on his face. "Can I sit?"

She moved over. His scent filled her nostrils— soap and aftershave—and brought back so many associations, she had to steel herself.

He asked, "How are you?"

"I'm so worried about Janey. Dan, what will we do if they bring her to trial?"

"Stand by her like you've been doing. Like Brad is doing." He closed his eyes, and she knew what he was thinking. *Like I didn't do for you.*

"Don't go there. It won't help anything."

"I know. I've wanted to apologize again for all that I did to you, but you won't see me. So let me say it now. I'm so sorry."

His words came back to her. *You think sorry is enough here?*

"Apology accepted."

His hand moved to take hers, but she pulled away from him.

He sat with her and Brad until eleven forty-five, when Janey came bursting out of the courtroom. She threw herself into her husband's arms. "They believed me!"

"Oh, Janey." Brad started to cry.

Janey started to cry.

But Tessa didn't. She rose and crossed to them. Janey hugged her and thanked her for everything she'd done in the past few days.

Grinning, Brad kept an arm around Janey. "Let's go celebrate."

"Let's," Janey agreed.

Janey didn't notice Dan until he stood. Tessa hoped she wasn't mean to him. He was in bad shape as it was.

"I'm glad it turned out this way, Janey."

"I'm sorry I didn't come forth sooner. I'll never forgive myself for that."

"Well, I'll never forgive myself for how I reacted when you first told us." He glanced at Tessa. "For a lot of things."

Janey hugged him and he held her close.

"So?" she said, turning to Tessa. "Mind if Dan comes along to celebrate?"

Tessa did mind. Now that Janey was free, she was going to have to deal with her husband. And her life. But she didn't want to do that yet. Today was for celebrating. "Sure, if that's what you want."

She saw the hurt in Dan's blue eyes but forced herself to ignore it. She grasped Janey's hand and started down the hall, with Dan taking up the rear.

CHAPTER SEVENTEEN

THE BAR, A RESTAURANT that catered to the law community in Orchard Place, resembled a courtroom with its wood paneling and chunky furniture. The place was crowded today, but Dan found Allison at a table near the back. He'd asked her to lunch to thank her for all she'd done for him. And to make it clear they didn't have a future together.

As he walked through the dining room, he noticed that she was wearing pearls with her purple suit. Pearls, like the ones Tessa had pawned to pay off Frankie.

"Hey, handsome. Nice suit."

"Thanks." He took a seat opposite her. He hadn't worn formal clothes in weeks, and it felt right to be back in them. He wasn't, however, back in his old skin.

"Thanks for taking me to lunch, though I have a feeling I'm not going to hear what I want to hear."

"Probably not." After ordering a club soda with lemon, Dan shook out his napkin and placed it on his lap. "There's no future for us outside of being friends and colleagues, Allison."

She set down her menu. Her nails were painted a bright red, and her makeup was flawless. She was every inch sophistication and upper class. None of which affected him in the least. "I'm sorry to hear that. How's it going with Tessa?"

He thought of the family dinners that were tolerable when the girls were with them, but as soon as he and Tessa were alone the air crackled with the strain. Tessa was still sleeping in the guest room, even though he'd tried exchanging rooms with her.

"Nothing I don't deserve."

"Is she staying with you?"

He set down his drink. "I have no idea."

"Are you sure there's no chance for us then?"

"No, I'm sorry. I can't tell you how much I appreciate your legal, emotional and financial support during the past few weeks. But…"

"You're in love with your wife. You always have been. And these past few weeks didn't change that."

"Not on my end, anyway."

"I'll get over it." She sipped her wine and gave him a pointed look. "Bet you wish you'd listened to me about being nicer to her."

"More than I can say." He cleared his throat, unable to discuss Tessa with her. "There's something else. Something professional I think we need to talk about."

"What?"

"I've been wondering, since I've been back to work, how I'm going to face you across a courtroom again. I'm not sure I can be cutthroat enough in legal negotiations after what you did for me."

Allison laughed, and he was glad to hear it. "Could be a problem. Maybe Karen and I can go at it. How is it at work?"

"Different. A lot of legal eagles have called to say they were glad I was back. But there's talk, and some people snub me. I'm sure there's a string of defense attorneys snickering all the time now."

"Pretty tough for someone who prided himself on his reputation."

"I can't say I like it. But it isn't the end of the world. Loss of respectability pales in comparison to what else I've lost."

"You know, if you ditched Tessa, you could regain the respect you once had in the legal community. Your actions would indicate that Tessa caused this whole thing and you did nothing wrong. And you'd no longer be associated with her checkered past." She hesitated. "It would be like what happened with your father, where you were the innocent victim. You were able to overcome that blight."

"I'm not abandoning Tessa to fend for herself in this city. I'll only leave her if she kicks me out."

Allison shook her head. "Your choice." She nodded to the menu. "Let's order."

After lunch, Dan decided not to go back to the office. He had an urge to see his daughters. They were with his mother right now, so he headed over to her condo complex to spend a couple of hours with them.

He called Claire's cell and she told him they were at the pool. At least his kids were having some fun this summer. As they'd expected, other children had not been kind. He pulled into the small parking lot near the pool, shed his suit coat and tie and grabbed his sunglasses. He spotted his mother in a lawn chair. She wore a big straw hat that shaded her eyes as she watched the water, where he assumed his children were playing.

Kissing her on the cheek, he dropped into a chair. "Hi, Mom."

"Hi, Dan." She took his hand; he appreciated her motherly affection. "I can't believe you're here in the middle of the day. I was afraid something was wrong when you called to say you were taking the afternoon off."

"I know. I would never have done something like this before. More's the pity."

"What do you mean by that?"

"The job, my work, has taken too much precedence in my life." He scanned the area for his kids. "They should have been my priority. And Tessa."

"I won't let you say you weren't a good father, Dan."

"No. But I could have spent more time with my children and my wife." He zeroed in on the diving board, where Molly waved before she did a cannonball into the water. "I missed seeing little things like this."

"Most working parents do. You can change that, though. It's not too late."

"For that, no."

She squeezed his hand. "It isn't any better with Tessa?"

"Each day she puts more distance between us. I'm afraid she's preparing me for a permanent split."

"I'm sorry."

"Have you talked to her, Mom?"

"Not about you. She's nice of course, and polite, but distant with me, too. It's like she's shutting herself off. Closing others out."

"That's how she was when I first met her. It took me years to get her to open up." He watched Sara go down the slide.

"I hope she comes out of it." When Dan didn't respond, she added, "Give her time."

"Yeah, sure." But his mother's encouragement didn't make him feel better.

Claire shifted in her seat. "Dan, I want to tell you something, and I hope it doesn't upset you more. Your father called me."

He whipped off his sunglasses and stared at her. "What?"

"He read about what happened to you. He was concerned."

Today, in the sunshine and amid the muck his own life had become, his anger toward his father felt less virulent. "Did he say anything else?"

"No, just that he was sorry for everything."

"Where is he?"

"He moved to a small town outside of Rockford. He has a reputable job earning enough money to offer me some. I've decided to take it, so you don't have to help support me anymore."

At one time, Dan would have thrown a fit if his mother wanted to have any kind of connection with his father. Now, he realized she had to live her own life as she saw fit, without his interference. It baffled him how much he had tried to control everything in the past.

"All right, if that's what you want. I'm surprised you'd take his money, though."

"When he put it in terms of having blown all our savings to cover up the embezzling and said I'd have gotten half of those savings when I divorced him, I decided to take what he was offering now."

Sara came barreling toward him, her nose sunburned, her little body dripping wet. She threw herself into his arms. "Dad-dy. What are you *doing* here in the daytime?"

"Taking a few hours to see my daughters."

"Where's Mom?"

"I'm not sure. She had some things to do today."

Molly came running to hug Dan, too. "Dad, you're all wet."

His trousers and shirt were damp. He remembered being annoyed when the kids mussed his clothes in the past. Even those had to be perfect.

"So? Hugs from my two favorite girls are worth a bit of wrinkling."

Molly eyed him. "Mommy's not your favorite anymore, is she?"

He swallowed hard. "Of course she is."

"Nuh-uh. You don't kiss and hug like you used to."

"Sure we do. In private." That was an outright lie. There had been no intimacy at all between them.

Just then, two boys walked by. About ten or twelve, they snorted and made rude noises. When they saw Molly and Sara, they said loud enough so everyone could hear them, "*Con-vict* girls."

Sara recoiled and Dan grabbed for her.

Molly's face flushed; she took a step toward the retreating boys and called out, "Go drown yourself, assholes!"

"Molly, don't use that language."

Knowing eyes leveled on him. "They say nasty things about Mom. I hate them."

He drew her into his arms with Sara. "I'm sorry, girls."

In the bright sunlight, he took no pleasure in their hugs. Coming face-to-face with what they were dealing with, he wanted to bawl like a baby.

"WE HAVE A NEW MEMBER today." The person who ran the group for women who had been in prison smiled over at Tessa. "Tessa, would you like to introduce yourself?"

She scanned the faces of the twelve women in the circle. They ranged in age from twenty to fifty; some were dressed well, some in jeans, some in tattered clothing. They spanned diverse racial backgrounds. And they'd all spent time in prison. "I don't think I need to tell you who I am. My name and face have been plastered all over the newspapers. I'm sure you know my crimes."

"Gotta say 'em anyway," a young black woman with cornrows told her. "It's part of the program."

Drawing in a breath, Tessa nodded. "I went to prison for the death of two people. It was a drunk-driving accident."

"You drivin'?" another woman asked. She had sad eyes but a kind smile.

"No. I was in the car. But I was drunk, and we had drugs in our possession."

"Thank the Lord you weren't behind the wheel," a woman with a Bible said. "I was drivin' in my accident. I'll never forgive myself." She held up the book. "Hope God will."

Tessa went on to explain the most recent turn of events.

"Sounds to me like you paid for your sins, girl," another woman commented.

"My husband and kids are feeling the fallout from those sins, I'm afraid. It's hard to forgive myself when a lot of innocent people are still suffering."

"That isn't your fault. We live in a judgmental society that refuses to let people make a clean start."

"Way to go, professor."

The moderator gestured to the articulate, smartly dressed woman who'd spoken. "This is Lena Michaels, a college professor at UB."

Tessa looked at the woman. "I killed my husband because he wouldn't stop beating up me and my children."

"I'm so sorry."

"I'm sorry he's dead. But he could have killed my sons, and I had to stop him. As it is, I'm afraid the abuse has done irreparable damage to them. I should have got them, and myself, out of the situation sooner."

The time passed with similar confessions and shared hope for the future. As she listened to the others' stories, she thanked her lucky stars Nick had convinced her to come here to work out her own issues.

At the end of the two hours, Tessa stayed back and talked to some of the women. By the time she got home, it was after noon. The girls were with her mother-in-law, who had been a pillar of strength for them all. Who would have thought Claire had that in her?

Alone in the house, Tessa went into the den to use the computer. She needed a job and was searching online for possibilities. Not long after Janey's confession, Tessa had received a stiff, formal letter saying that due to her absence from work, the library had found someone to replace her. They were sorry, but they had no job for her to return to. Reading between the lines wasn't difficult. The town, which ran the library, didn't want someone like her working for them.

Before she went on the job Web site, she called up her e-mail.

There were no answers to her previous job queries. But there was Dan's daily e-mail. For some reason, he'd taken to contacting her like this. He'd ask about her day, what the girls were doing and give her his schedule. The missives were chatty and low key.

And she loved them. When she and Dan were together, they couldn't talk about anything. Everyday occurrences that they had once shared. And of course, big things. He couldn't find words to express his remorse, and she couldn't find words to tell him it was over.

Today's e-mail ended with, "I love you, Tessa. I'm not sure you love me anymore, because I don't even love myself. I'll do anything I can to make all this up to you. Please."

He concluded each e-mail with some version of that statement. She swallowed hard, treasuring the precious words. And then she hit the Delete button.

She went back to the job Web site and found a new ad. Librarian Needed at St. James Villa, Rockford, New York.

She clicked onto their Web site. St. James Villa was a residential home for juveniles who'd been in detention centers or who had avoided incarceration by being sent to the facility. Tessa read about its history and philosophy. She checked the pay scale. It was decent. But the job was full-time. And it was in Rockford.

Well, maybe fate was helping her out. She'd loved working with Nick's kids, and working in the villa would be similar to what she'd been doing with the center.

And there was something else, some other reason to consider this job. Though she'd been toying with the idea since Janey was acquitted, Lena Michael's statement hours ago had crystallized it for her. *I'm afraid the abuse has done irreparable damage to the kids. I should have got them, and myself, out of the situation sooner.*

Tessa should move the girls out of Orchard Place. And to do that, she'd need a full-time job with benefits. After studying the villa's Web site, she hit the button to bring up the application. Then she printed it out.

DAN SAT UP IN BED, pretending interest in the ten o'clock news, but his mind kept wandering to the printout he'd discovered on the desk when he'd got home that day. It was an application for a librarian's job. In a different city. His lungs had felt like they were collapsing in his chest as the meaning sunk in. He intended to ask Tessa about it—he wasn't letting her go without a fight—but he wanted to think it through first. No more going off half-cocked about anything.

There was a knock at the bedroom door, then it opened and Tessa peeked inside. "Can I come in? I need some cream from the vanity drawer. My hands are chapped from digging in the dirt with Janey."

"Of course you can come in." He hated that she knocked on her own bedroom door.

She was dressed in red cotton pajamas with black hearts on them. The top had spaghetti straps and the bottoms only came to her knees. She looked about twenty in the outfit, with her hair up in some kind of clip. Walking past him, she left a whiff of lilacs in her wake.

When she came out of the bathroom, he grabbed her hand. "Sit down for a minute, would you?" He slid over to make room.

"I'm not sure…"

"Please, I need to talk about a couple of things."

With a sigh, she sat. "If it's about the girls, I know they're getting grief around the neighborhood. We have to do something about it."

He cleared his throat. "Is that why you're looking at jobs in another city?" At her raised eyebrows, he said, "I found the application you downloaded from the Internet on my desk. I swear I wasn't prying or keeping track of you."

"I should have been more careful."

"What does it mean, Tessa?"

Her eyes filled with resignation. "That we have to make some decisions here, Dan. We can't keep living in this limbo."

"Let's end this limbo, then. Give me another chance, and we'll make those decisions together. What's best for all of us."

"I'm not sure I can make plans with you."

"Are you going to leave me?"

"I don't know."

Instead of protesting, he took the tube of cream out of her hands and removed the top. He put a dab on his fingers and picked up her right hand. Finger by slender finger, her rubbed the cream on her dry skin. She sucked in a breath as he massaged it into her palm. He lifted her other hand and kissed her wedding band. At least she was still wearing it. When he raised his gaze to hers, she was glassy-eyed.

He'd never wanted her more.

Putting additional cream on his fingers, he smoothed the lotion on her throat. He'd seen her do this ritual a million times and knew it by heart. When his hands strayed to the top of her pj's, she stayed them.

"Dan, don't."

"Please, let me touch you. I won't go any further than you want."

"You…I thought you'd never want to touch me again." Her voice was raw. "After you found out I was in jail. You went on those Web sites…"

"I was out of my mind. I can't bear the thought that you might have been abused in prison."

"You wouldn't see me as tainted if something happened?"

"Of course not. I'd cry for you."

"I—"

He put his fingers to her lips. "You don't have to tell me. Just know where I was coming from. Please, if nothing else, believe this one thing."

She gripped his wrists, and instead of pushing him away she held on tight. "All right. I believe that."

His eyes closed in relief, and she dropped her hands. Taking the tube from him, she capped it and started to stand.

"Wait, just one more thing."

She stayed where she was as he pulled out the nightstand drawer and lifted out a jeweler's box.

Her gaze narrowed on the red velvet, but she said nothing. He opened it and took out the strand of pearls he'd put in it earlier.

"Oh, Dan, no. I don't want new pearls. It wouldn't be the same, and in any case—"

"They aren't new."

"What?"

"They're the ones I gave you on your wedding day, when I promised to love you no matter what. I know I broke that promise. But I wanted you to have these back."

"How did you get them?"

"When you hock something, sweetheart, you have a certain number of days to retrieve it. I found the receipt you left on our dresser and went to Niagara to get these."

"When?"

"Today."

"Oh, Dan. I can't believe you did this. I don't know what to say."

"I'm not bribing you with them. No matter what you decide, I want you to have them."

"All right."

With all the tenderness she deserved, he slipped the pearls around her throat and clasped them. Reverently he kissed her forehead. "I will never let you down again. I've learned you are the most precious thing in my life." In case she didn't understand, he whispered, "I love you. Please, don't leave me. Give me another chance."

He felt her body shake. She was crying.

That was okay, because so was he.

CHAPTER EIGHTEEN

HOT END-OF-JUNE SUNSHINE beat down on Janey and Tessa as they lounged in the water chairs Brad had bought for Janey on her birthday. Today she and her sister looked even more alike in hot-pink racing suits. Janey's hair was up in a knot, which made her look young. Since she'd already gone swimming, Tessa's curls were all over the place.

Eyes closed, face turned up to the hot rays, Janey moved her hand back and forth in the water. "So, are you going to tell me about the pearls?"

Tessa traced the tiny white beads she hadn't been able to take off since Dan gave them to her a few days ago. She filled Janey in on how she'd pawned them and how Dan had redeemed them for her. She couldn't picture her staid husband going into a pawn shop. But maybe he wasn't so staid anymore. Since Frankie had been killed, they were all different, but Dan's changes were the most striking.

Tears leaked from Janey's eyes. Tessa watched them track down her cheeks.

"Oh, honey, don't cry." There had been too many waterworks in their lives of late.

"I keep thinking if I hadn't killed Frankie, you and Dan would be together. Have you told him you're leaving?"

"Not yet. I can't get the words out."

Her sister looked over at her. "What does that tell you, Tess?"

"That it breaks my heart to end our marriage. That I can't imagine my life without him."

"Dan wants to stay together."

"We've hurt each other too much. He thinks he can forgive what I did to his reputation, but I don't see that he can." She took a deep breath. "And, truthfully, I've been trying to forget the awful things he said to me, the disgusted way he looked at me, but when I go to sleep, or even let my mind wander, it all comes back."

"He knows you're hurting."

"Have you talked to him?"

"No, but Dan and Brad had lunch yesterday, and they spent the afternoon together."

"Didn't either of them have to work?"

Without answering, Janey rolled off the chair into the water. That was odd.

When she surfaced, she said, "This feels great. Come in."

"In a minute. What's going on with Brad?"

Janey's lashes were spiky from the pool. They

couldn't hide the concern in her eyes. "I think he's getting grief about the grant. Because of me."

"Oh, God, that's the last straw. First Dan, then our kids, then your kids. Now Brad is paying for what I did?"

"No, Tessa. Brad's paying for what *I* did. And I wish you'd stop taking the blame for everything." Her forceful tone had Tessa reeling back. "Honestly, it makes me feel worse."

"Worse, why?"

"Because I don't feel as remorseful as you do."

"What?"

"Don't get me wrong. I feel bad that Brad's having trouble at work and the boys are being taunted by their classmates. But I killed Frankie in self-defense, and though I'm sorry he's dead, because he was so mixed up, I'm not sorry I stopped him from hurting me." She added, "Or you."

Tessa didn't know what to say. Janey's outburst surprised her.

She wasn't done. "And now you keep taking the blame for it all. It makes what I did senseless. We're all suffering with no real relief in sight because your marriage is breaking up over this."

Tessa stared at Janey. "I—I don't know what to say."

Janey swam to the side of the pool and levered herself up to sit on the edge. Tessa slid off the chair and dove underwater to the side. When she surfaced, she hung on to the concrete, looking up at her sister.

"Do you blame me for not telling you sooner?" Janey asked. "For not coming right home from London when I found out Frankie died? For getting Dan arrested?"

"No. You were acting out of fear and anger and confusion."

"So you forgive me? For acting out of fear and anger and confusion."

"Yes, of course."

"Then do us all a favor and forgive Dan. Because he acted out of those things, too. He was very wrong to treat you as he did, but he's a human being with flaws. You have to forgive him, because if you two split over what's happened, then that's the biggest tragedy."

When Tessa returned home to fix dinner, Nick's car pulled into the driveway behind hers. Afraid she was going to get pressured by her brother-in-law, Tessa tried to head it off. "If you're here on Dan's behalf, I don't want to talk about him."

"I'm not." He leaned over and kissed her cheek, pulling her close. His hug lasted longer than usual.

In the kitchen, he dropped into a chair, and she noticed he was holding his cell phone in his left hand. "Would you like to stay for dinner?"

"Not on your life. Eating supper here is like picking through a minefield." He nodded to the fridge. "I'd take some lemonade, though."

As she removed a can of concentrate from the freezer and found a pitcher in the cupboard, he said,

"The reason I don't want to stay for dinner is the reason I came over."

Here it comes. She turned to the sink and placed the frozen can in the basin. "You said you didn't come to defend Dan."

"I didn't. I came to ask you to leave Dan and marry me."

Tessa dropped the glass pitcher in the sink. It shattered. She spun around. Nick was sitting all lazylike in jeans and T-shirt, with a sneakered foot resting on his knee. "What did you say?"

"I'm in love with you, Tessa, and I think you care about me. Be with me. I'll take care of you and the kids."

"How can you ask me that?" she said angrily. "How can you even consider doing something like that to your own brother? It would *kill* Dan. He doesn't deserve your betrayal. He needs your loyalty, now especially, when things are so bad between us."

"I don't care what Dan needs. I only care about you."

"Well *I* care." She pushed the tangled mass of her hair off her face. "If I ever left Dan, I'd never marry again. No man could ever replace him."

Nick arched an eyebrow, seemingly unmoved by her words. "Really?"

"I know you feel affection for me, Nick, but you're not in love with me." She studied his face, which was unreadable. "I know you aren't."

He waited a beat. "You're right, Tessa, I'm not in love with you."

She stilled. "Then why did you say you were?"

"Because I wanted to force *you* to say out loud what you just did. I wanted you to make the choice you just made."

She frowned at him.

"You love Dan. You'd never do anything to hurt him. You might leave him, thinking it's for his own welfare or believing you could never make it work for you as a couple, but you're wrong." He held up what she thought earlier was his cell phone.

"What the hell is that?"

"I recorded what you said, for you to play back. Listen to this until you get it through your head that you're still crazy about your husband and should give him another chance." With an odd smile on his face, he crossed and kissed her forehead. "Let me correct myself. I do love you, Tessa. Like a sister. Don't let me down."

When he left, she sputtered after him, then went to the table and picked up the device he'd left there. Sure enough, it was a tape recorder. The devil. Still, she pressed the button to rewind.

And then she pressed Play.

DAN CAME HOME EARLY from the office and found Tessa at the computer. He stood in the doorway, watching her scroll down the screen.

"Hi, Tessa."

She looked up. "Hi."

"Have a good day?"

She rolled her eyes. "It was interesting."

"Want to tell me?"

"No, not now." She studied him. "You look dead on your feet."

"I am. Rough day in the office." He hastened to add, "Not because of you."

She nodded.

"Did I see the glass pitcher in the garbage?"

"I, um, broke it making lemonade."

"Oh, I'm sorry. It was a wedding gift."

"I remember."

"I guess there's a lot more broken than that." She started to speak, and he held up his hand. "No, I don't mean to keep bringing this up." He glanced at his watch. "I'm going for a run."

"All right. If you see the girls at the park, tell them to get home by five. We're having chicken for dinner."

"Sounds good." His stomach felt sick all the time, like it was on rinse cycle.

"Dan?"

He looked back at her.

"You've got to take better care of yourself."

"Yeah, sure, I will."

He started by blanking his mind and running around the park's path with his demons on his heels.

Then he pushed the kids on the swings and felt somewhat better. When he returned home, he took a shower. Before he came downstairs, the doorbell rang. Tessa reached the foyer ahead of him. He was on the steps when she opened the door.

She cocked her head at the person on the front stoop. "Can I help you?"

"Hello, Tessa."

She stumbled back, and her shoulders stiffened as if she was afraid. When the news had broken about Hamilton's death, reporters had come to the house and hounded them. Prepared to do battle, Dan trundled down the last few steps and into view. He put his hand on his wife's shoulder and looked past her—into the face of his father.

SITTING CLOSE TO DAN on the couch, Tessa took his hand in hers. It was ice-cold. Daniel, Sr. sat across from them. Her husband linked their fingers and held on tightly.

"You're wondering why I'm here." His father's voice was flat, matter-of-fact. Dan resembled him in looks, but not in gestures, or even the way he held himself. Tessa had seen a picture of Daniel; he'd aged. His hair was now white and thinning. His blue eyes had dulled.

Dan said, "Yes, of course we are."

"I know your mother told you I called. I heard what happened."

Untangling his hand, Dan slipped his arm around Tessa. "If you've come about Tessa, I warn you now, I'll physically remove you from my home if you say one negative word about her."

"That's not why I came. I've kept track of you and Nick. I know you've spent the years living down my legacy, and Nick's spent them defying it. I can't tell you how much it pains me to see what I've done to you." He nodded to Tessa. "And to you."

"We're coping," Dan told his father. "And Nick's made something of himself."

"I know. I'm proud of both of you."

"Not much to be proud of with me right now." The words tumbled out of Dan's mouth and he winced, as if he hadn't meant to say them.

"Dan, don't."

"What do you mean, Danny? You were innocent."

"I didn't handle things well when the Hamilton case broke."

"No?"

"No." Briefly, he glanced at Tessa. "And I can't make it right."

"I know something about that."

Dan studied his father for several moments. "I never let you make things right. Me or Nick. Or Mom."

"I didn't deserve a chance anyway."

Dan knew *that* feeling.

The back door banged, and Sara and Molly called out, "Mom, Dad…"

Tessa rose to quiet them as they slid to a halt in the doorway. Looking like imps with dirty faces and grass-stained clothes, they took in the adults.

Molly said, "What are you doing in here?"

"Who is that man, Daddy?" Sara asked.

Dan stared at his father for long, uncomfortable moments. Even the girls waited with uncustomary patience.

"Girls, I want you to meet my father. Dad, this is Molly and Sara, my daughters."

Tessa's eyes blurred.

"This is our *grandpa?*" Molly asked, wide-eyed.

"How come we never met him before, Daddy?" Sara wanted to know.

Swallowing hard, Daniel stood. "Because I did some bad things and had to go away for a long time."

"And—" his son put in "—because I couldn't forgive him."

Molly looked to Tessa. "That's not right, is it, Mom? You said we have to forgive people when they hurt us."

Tessa stared at all of them blankly.

THE NEXT AFTERNOON, Tessa was running a bath with scented bubbles and had just gotten a change of clothes out of the dresser when the phone rang. She hoped it wasn't Dan calling to say he was going to be late from work. She snatched up the receiver. "Hello?"

"So, are you wearing it?"

"Not yet. I'm taking a bath."

Janey laughed on the other end. "This is déjà vu, isn't it?"

Tessa chuckled. "Not really. We're not the same people we were on our anniversary. None of us."

"Your relationship will be better now, honey. I know."

"I agree. Gotta go. The bath's filling. Tell the girls to behave."

Tessa hung up and walked to her bathroom, took off her clothes and slipped into the steaming water. The bath oil was new and smelled sinful.

So much had happened since her anniversary two months ago. It seemed like a lifetime had passed. Tessa felt better now that there were no secrets waiting to spring out of the closet. And she knew in her heart she and Dan could make a go of it, if they tried. She had yet to tell him she wasn't leaving, though. She'd wanted to do it in a special way.

After the girls had met his father, Dan asked him to stay for dinner. Then Dan and he had spent the evening in the den. They'd called Nick, but he wouldn't come over. Daniel, Sr. left late, and Dan had been so whipped, he'd fallen into bed exhausted. Tessa had lain awake for hours in the spare room thinking things through. By morning, she'd made some decisions.

Her head back, she hummed to the rock music she'd put on the stereo and sipped her champagne.

The bath was long and luxurious; she was dressed and waiting for him when she heard the door to the garage entrance slam.

Dan burst into the kitchen with a vigor he hadn't had in weeks. It had taken him all day to set things in motion, but he had, damn it, and now he was going to tell Tessa. This time, he wouldn't take no for an answer. If he could begin to accept his father again, he could damn well convince his wife to stay with him. Carrying the bright yellow daisies he'd bought her, along with two envelopes, he dropped his briefcase on the floor, went to the stairway and yelled, "Tessa, where are you?"

"Up here."

He took the steps two at a time. Long strides got him to the doorway of the bedroom, where he came to an abrupt halt. He did a double take. She was in their bed, where she hadn't been in weeks, dressed in that sexy black thing Janey had given her to wear on their anniversary. He wanted to drop down on his knees and thank God that he might not have to bulldoze her into staying with him.

"Hi."

Her smile was beautiful. She made quite a picture, leaning back against the snowy-white pillowcase, her curly hair spread over it. "Hi."

"You…you look gorgeous. And sexy as hell."

Fiddling with the strap of the top, she let one fall off her shoulder. "Not too risqué?"

He said what was on his heart. "Thank God, I think we're past all that."

She smiled. "I'm glad. Dan, I—"

"No, me first." He strode to the bed and sank down beside her. Because he couldn't stop himself, he leaned over and kissed the pearls at her neck. "Oh, God. You smell so good. New perfume?"

"Bath oil." She grasped his shoulders. "Dan."

"No wait." Drawing back, he handed her the flowers.

"Daisies," she said burying her face in them.

"I thought we'd try something different." A lot of things different. Everything different.

"Good idea." She nodded to the two envelopes he carried. "What are those?"

He placed them in her other hand. "Look."

After she set the daisies aside, she opened the first and scanned it. "What?" Her expression was puzzled. "Dan, why on earth did you get me an interview at St. Joseph's Villa next week?"

"Because you're perfect for the job. A librarian for all those troubled kids. You'll be great for them."

Her eyes clouded. "It's in Rockford. I don't understand, I thought…"

His fingers on her mouth hushed her. "Look in the other envelope."

Her hands were shaky as she removed the paper and read it. Her eyebrows shot up. "No, Dan, no, I won't let you do this."

KATHRYN SHAY   295

"It's already done. That's a copy. I handed the original in to the mayor before I left work today."

"Why did you resign from the D.A.'s office?"

"Because I want to start over. Where people aren't saying nasty things to you or the girls, or to me for that matter. Where no one will look down on you because you made a mistake." He brushed back her hair and took a second to wind a curl around his finger. "Don't get me wrong. We won't hide anything. I just want a clean slate where I don't have to be Saint Daniel."

"Oh, Dan." She hated to leave Janey and Nick and Claire. But she knew in her heart Dan was right about moving. It was perfect.

He started to yank off his tie. "There's more. But I hope you don't mind, I'm going to get undressed as I tell you." The tie hit the floor. It was joined by his suit coat jacket. "I've already gotten Mom in on this. She's going to move to Rockford, too."

"What? Slow down, you're going too fast."

He ripped the buttons of his shirt. "Holy hell, this isn't fast *enough*. I have to have you. Right away."

She giggled like a girl when he snatched a wet, open-mouthed kiss. Without reservation, she returned it. "What about a job for you?"

"I figured that out, too. I think. God, yes, I did. I contacted Jay Smith. You remember my college roommate from our trip to Rockford?" Bare-chested now, he leaned over and whispered, "You remember

Belhurst Castle. Tonight's going to be even more wild, love."

She closed her eyes while he kissed her throat. "Dan, your job."

"Yeah. Right. Jay's ready for a partner. His firm does a lot of pro bono work so I won't make a ton of money, but with any luck you'll be working, too, at the villa."

Kicking off his shoes—one hit the wall and the other fell into the pile of clothes on the floor—he reached for his belt, dragged down his zipper. "This is the best part."

She gave him a saucy wink. "I know it is, big guy."

"No. Not that. Thanks, though." Leaning over, he fondled her breast—jeez he couldn't stop touching her—then he put his hand on the waistband of his trousers and briefs. "Brad and I talked all morning. He says he might want to leave his practice here in town. He hates that people are nasty to Janey and the boys. He'd already started looking around for a new job. There's this great research university in Rockford, associated with Strong Memorial Hospital. He thinks they'd take him."

"Dan, you know what? Shut up now. Okay? And take off your pants."

He didn't realize sexual teasing could be so much fun. "One more thing. We'll have to work on Nick to come along. He lived in Rockford before he came back here, so it might not be too hard—"

She reached out and grabbed his waistband. "Speaking of hard…"

He dropped the rest of his clothes, slid her over on the bed and covered her silk-clad body with his naked one. "I'm so hot to have you I can't think straight." He buried his face in her neck and reached down for her panties. They ripped. "Oh. God. Hell. Tessa. I'm crazy for you."

She bit his shoulder. "Ah, I like hearing that."

"I love you, Tessa, more now than ever."

He could tell by the look in her eyes that she knew exactly what he meant, that he accepted her for who she was and had been.

"Nothing could mean more to me than that."

And then he kissed her.

HARLEQUIN® *Romance*

A family saga begins to unravel
when the doors to the Bella Lucia
Restaurant Empire are opened...

The Brides of Bella Lucia

*A family torn apart by secrets,
reunited by marriage*

AUGUST 2006

Meet Rachel Valentine, in
HAVING THE FRENCHMAN'S BABY
by Rebecca Winters

Find out what happens when a night of passion is followed
by a shocking revelation and an unexpected pregnancy!

SEPTEMBER 2006

The Valentine family saga continues with
THE REBEL PRINCE by Raye Morgan

Stability is highly overrated....

Dana Logan's world had always revolved around her children. Now they're all grown up and don't seem to need anything she's able to give them. Struggling to find her new identity, Dana realizes that it's about time for her to get "off her rocker" and begin a new life!

Off Her Rocker

by Jennifer Archer

Available August 2006
TheNextNovel.com

HN53

HARLEQUIN®

Next™

Silhouette

Desire

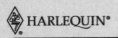